By Sophie Snow

TOUCH AND GO SERIES

The Rule of Three

• • •

SPICY IN SEATTLE SERIES

Legally Binding

False Confidence

Dearly Unbeloved

• • •

WINTERMORE SERIES

Naughty or Nice

Spicy or Sweet

Fall or Fly

spicy or sweet

SOPHIE SNOW

To everyone giving their blood, sweat, and tears to make their dreams come true.

And to you, reading this, for making mine come true.

Content Warnings

Spicy or Sweet is an adult novel that features explicit content and some topics that may be triggering for some readers. The following is a list of topics featured in Spicy or Sweet:

Car Accident (described in detail), claustrophobia, death of a sibling (described in detail), divorce (in past), explicit language, explicit sexual content (fingering, food play, masturbation (solo), masturbation (mutual), oral sex, penetration with a non-toy, penetration with a strap-on, sex toys), fire, grief, homophobia (past), hospitals, injury, job pressure, panic attack, pregnancy (side characters), questioning/struggling with Queer identity, smoke inhalation.

You can read about these content warnings in more detail at www. sophiesnowbooks.com.

1
NOELLE

Nobody warned me that adulthood is just an endless stream of dirty dishes.

Sure, I expected there to be a lot of dishes when I opened my bakery—I even hired someone specifically to keep on top of them—but the sheer volume is staggering. Since opening The Enchanted Bakery last Christmas, I've had to hire a second dishwasher, and even then, I'm here after closing most days, washing up.

And when it's not dishes, it's laundry. Or spraying down the surfaces. Or deep-cleaning the fridge. Or brushing leaves off the sidewalk and tables outside. God, there are so many leaves.

My hometown of Wintermore, Wyoming, is best known as the backdrop of the best-selling holiday movie, *A Christmas Wish in the Mountains*. Every year, a perfect dusting of snow covers the town, and tourists from all over flock to visit. My family loves Christmas more than most—we moved here *because* it's a Christmas town—but I love fall almost as much.

It's the anticipation: the crunch of the first crispy leaf; the day you open your eyes and the world looks a little more warm-toned; the transition from T-shirts to light cardigans to thick sweaters. In my family, winter has always been the busiest time of year. Fall is the season when everything changes—the calm before the storm.

Or it was, anyway. These days, I wouldn't know calm if it hit me over the head with a rolling pin.

I rinse the last stainless steel mixing bowl, holding it up to the light to make sure there's no residual butter, and set it on the drying rack. The stack of now-clean dishes is too big to leave for the morning, but the thought of drying them and putting them all away after the day I've had makes me want to break something. I dry my hands on my apron, cursing as powdered sugar sticks to them, and turn away from the sink.

The fading glow of the sunset shines through the windows as I pull off my apron, ball it up, and toss it in the hamper. Putting away the dishes, laundry, unpacking this afternoon's delivery… I'm going to be pissed at myself in the morning when I have to wake up an hour earlier than my usual five a.m. to get everything done. But I've been here for thirteen hours and barely stopped. I need a break.

Apartments in Wintermore are hard to come by, but most of the stores in the town square have upstairs apartments. Thank god —if I had to commute, I'd probably end up curling up in the storage room in the basement every night. My apartment is cozy and homey—considering how little time I spend there—but I don't want to be in this building anymore.

I leave the back of the bakery, inspecting the front of the house and mentally adding to tomorrow's to-do list on my way out the door. It's still too warm in Wintermore for a jacket, but the breeze is cool enough to wake me up a little. I lock the bakery door, turn around, and breathe it in. I can smell the change of the season in the air, but it doesn't bring me the sense of excitement it once did. Now, all I can think about is the hordes of tourists a month or two away from rushing into town, and how busy I'm going to be.

Closing my eyes, I force myself to focus on the soft sound of rustling leaves, the smell of sugar and ginger (that I'm pretty sure has more to do with me than the season), and the feel of the cool breeze tickling my neck. Slowly, the tension from the day starts to fade a little.

A soft jingle sounds, and I look across the street, every drop of tension flooding right back into my spine. Shay Harland exits her bakery—*patisserie*— lifting her hand and smiling as she waves.

"It's getting chilly," she calls, wrapping a maroon scarf around her. "Have a good night, Noelle!" She doesn't wait for me to respond before heading down the street—in the opposite direction I'm heading. Thank god.

I grit my teeth and start the other way. Of all the things that stress me about running my bakery, Shay is at the top of the list.

My family moved to Wintermore to open our toy store, The Enchanted Workshop, when I was seven, and I've always dreamed of opening a bakery here. There was an amazing bakery in my hometown in Texas before we moved here, and, though Wintermore has a couple of cafés and a ton of restaurants, I missed a true bakery growing up—somewhere with more exciting treats than basic chocolate chip cookies and vanilla cupcakes. I began saving my toy store wages as soon as my parents started paying me, and majored in business at college while taking pastry night classes at culinary school five days a week, so I'd be ready to put down a deposit and get started as soon as I came home.

Instead, I got stuck looking after The Enchanted Workshop for seven years because my older brother, Felix, couldn't take his job as manager seriously. Then four years ago, Shay arrived in Wintermore and stole my dream out from under me, opening *Épices et Sucré*, a.k.a. Spicy and Sweet.

And so began my four-year, one-sided feud with Shay Harland.

She calls it a patisserie, but it's just a slightly fancier than usual bakery. Her menu has become significantly less French-inspired as she's come to know the Wintermore market better. There were lines out the door when she opened, confirming what I always suspected: Wintermore was in dire need of a bakery. I shouldn't be surprised that someone else had the idea. If anything, I'm surprised it didn't happen earlier. Bakeries are a given in kitschy small towns like this. But the success of Shay's place had me questioning if Wintermore needed two. From my view, peering longingly out the window of the toy store I never wanted to run, it looked like she had the market covered.

I almost gave up entirely, but I kept saving, kept practicing, and when the owners of the coffee shop next to The Enchanted Workshop decided to retire somewhere sunny, I pounced.

Felix got his shit together and started pulling his weight, and the townsfolk have been nothing but supportive of my bakery, despite *Épices et Sucré* being just across the street. Almost *too* supportive, if I'm being honest. My hometown has shown up for me in droves, not to mention the tourists. Everything is perfect. And I hate it.

I know my work is excellent; it more than speaks for itself. But I'm also well aware that I owe a hell of a lot of my bakery's success to how well-liked my family is in Wintermore. My luck isn't lost on me, and I sound ungrateful as all hell, which is why, as far as everyone else is concerned, I'm having the time of my life. I'm no stranger to hard work, but this isn't what I expected. All I've ever wanted is to bake. I love the precision, the science, the art behind turning what looks like nothing into something incredible. But these days, I spend more time out front, talking to customers, doing admin, advertising, and doing all the other things that go along with running a business than I do in the kitchen. Some days, I don't even touch a spatula. It's a petty complaint in the grand scheme of things, but the pressure of owning a business and trying to keep everything together by myself is suffocating.

I hurry along the streets, chasing the sunset as I turn into the cul-de-sac I grew up in. I only moved out last year, and my parents still live here, but it's not their driveway I trudge up. My mom has been needling me and Felix to stop by more since we moved out, but I have no idea why. We both live less than five minutes away, and I swear my parents spend 90 percent of their days between The Enchanted Toy Store and The Enchanted Bakery. It's not like we don't see each other.

I knock twice, and a second later, my best friend pulls the door open.

"I need to cuddle the baby," I say before she can open her mouth.

Rora eyes my clothes with concern as I step into the living room. Or rather, she eyes the dusting of powdered sugar, butter stains, and orange marmalade covering me from head to toe. Fuck knows how they got past the apron, but they always do.

"It's after eight, Noelle."

"And? She's three months old. I know she's not sleeping."

Right on cue, my niece's happy little giggle sounds from the kitchen, and she appears in the doorway in the arms of her dad. The sound alone is enough to lift my spirits after the day from hell. Three months old, and Sunny has no idea about the horrors of customer service, taxes, or the goddamn price of butter. Oh, to be a clueless newborn.

"Gimme," I say, holding my arms out toward my uncle Henry —Sunny's dad, and Rora's boyfriend. It's been almost two years since my best friend asked me for permission to seduce my uncle, and saying yes might just be the best thing I've ever done. They're a perfect match, and they made a damn cute baby.

Uncle Henry snorts, but hands Sunny over. "Nice to see you too."

I ignore him, cuddling her to my chest and kissing the top of her head as I sink onto their plush couch. She babbles at me, and I melt. It's amazing how fast she's growing—a couple of weeks ago, she was silent. Now, she's cooing and giggling happily whenever I see her.

"And how is my favorite girl in the whole world tonight? Did you have a good day, Sunny girl?"

"I remember when I used to be your favorite," Rora says, sitting beside me and tucking her legs under herself.

I nod toward my uncle Henry. "You're his favorite now."

Rora looks fondly at him. "I reckon it's a tie between me and Sunny these days," she says before turning back to me. "You okay? You look tired."

"Of course. I'm fine!" I feign a bright smile—badly, if Rora's raised brow is anything to go by.

"Noelle."

"Ugh. How am I this much of a mess when you're so put together three months after giving birth?"

You'd never know Rora had a newborn. She's always had a seemingly effortlessly together vibe, and that hasn't changed since becoming a mom. She's as gorgeous as ever, looks perfectly rested, her green eyes bright and alert. I know it's probably not as it seems—raising a whole human is no easy feat, and I have no doubt her world shifted on its axis the second she got the positive test—but she's doing an amazing job. They both are—my uncle Henry's always wanted to be a dad, and he and Rora really are the perfect combination.

"Seriously, how are you both managing so well with everything?" I don't love how exhausted I sound. I squeeze Sunny a little tighter, breathing in her perfect, soft baby scent.

"We're not. Henry wakes up every hour through the night just to check that Sunny hasn't magically disappeared, I cry multiple times a day, and I go through a can of dry shampoo every week,"

Rora replies matter-of-factly, and I widen my eyes over the top of Sunny's head.

"But you seem so okay."

She shrugs. "I promise you don't want details of what we're doing for stress relief. But on that note, when was the last time you hooked up with someone?"

Jesus. Rora is nothing if not blunt—and correct. I don't want details.

"This feels like a conversation I don't want to be here for." My uncle Henry stands and reaches for Sunny, but I hold her close to my chest.

"It's girl talk. Sunny can stay."

He holds up his hands. "Noted. Did you eat dinner?"

"I'm fine," I answer immediately. I was lucky to make time for breakfast this morning.

"That's not a yes. I'm making food," he says, heading into the kitchen and ignoring my protests. God knows they have enough on their plate without worrying about me.

Rora nudges me with her foot. "Let him. He likes to fuss. Now talk. What's going on with you?"

I groan and lean back against the arm of the couch. Sunny nestles her head against my shoulder, her eyes drooping. She's so fucking cute.

"I'm just worn out." I'm underselling it, but I don't know how to describe the bone-deep burnout. "I'm working like a hundred hours a week, and I haven't taken time off in ages. And to answer your question: fuck knows when I last got laid. I haven't had time to go to Jackson in months." I'm not against meeting people in Wintermore, but this is a small town, and the number of queer women—let alone single queer women—is slim. Sure, tourists come and go, but it's not like I'm hanging out at either of the local bars. How would I meet someone?

"Maybe it's time to hire a couple new people for the bakery,"

Rora suggests, and I know she's right, but there are a finite number of people with experience in Wintermore. Besides, the thought of handing over control to anyone makes me itchy. I'm running out of other options, though. Especially with our busy season approaching.

"As for getting laid, it's the twenty-first century, Noelle. Download a dating app. You can either find tourists in town or match with people in Jackson who are willing to come here. It's not that far."

"I don't know. Aren't dating apps for dating? I don't have time for that."

"You can say on your profile that you're not looking to date. Give me your phone."

"Now?"

"The tension in your spine isn't healthy. We have to do something about it," Rora replies, shaking her head as I hand my phone over.

She types in my passcode: 1225—Christmas Day—and her tongue pokes out in concentration as she downloads the app and sets up my profile. I leave her to it, enjoying the almost-silence. The soft sounds of Sunny's tiny snores are better than any white noise machine, and I swear I'm drifting off when Rora sits up and declares my profile finished.

"It's nothing fancy, but it's not like you're itching for a marriage proposal," she says.

I take the phone, trying not to jostle Sunny, but she's a nosy little thing, and wakes up immediately, squinting at the phone light.

"Wow, sweet girl. I think we actually managed five whole minutes of sleep there," Rora says with an eye roll. Sunny babbles, seemingly wide awake. Babies.

Rora's done a good job with my profile. I can't deny that.

She's chosen a good mix of candid and casual pictures, and a few professional shots—courtesy of her. My bio and interests are vague, but not bare, and the prompts she selected all make it clear that I'm on the app for one thing and one thing only.

"How'd you get so good at this? You've never used a dating app."

"There's a British reality show about critiquing dating profiles, and I swear every airline has it available on the in-flight entertainment. I must have watched about three hundred episodes."

That's the last thing I expect her to say. I snort, swiping to the bottom of my profile. "Do I just hit the button?"

"Apparently. I set the location to eighty miles, so it should cover from here to Jackson," Rora says.

I shift the squirming baby in my arms so she's lying on her tummy across my lap, then set the phone on the couch between me and Rora before hitting the "let's go!" button.

All three of us peer at the spinning pink circle on the screen as it takes its sweet time looking for possible matches. I open my mouth to joke that there must not be anyone around, when a profile pops up on the screen.

"You've got to be kidding me."

Shay Harland's smug smile shines on my phone. Well, maybe not smug. She actually has a nice smile, but I need it not to be on my screen.

"Holy shit, what are the odds?" Rora's clearly fighting a laugh.

"I had no idea she was into women. She doesn't give that vibe."

"She totally gives that vibe, Noelle. You just refuse to talk to her. You know, she's really not that—" She stops talking, pressing her lips together when I glare at her.

"How do I say no?"

"I assume you swipe on the big red X on the screen."

I ignore her sarcastic tone, leaning closer to my phone, finger poised to say no fucking thank you. But Sunny gets there first, brandishing her tiny little fist toward the screen… and swiping the flashing green check mark.

2
SHAY

I've been doing this for long enough to know better than to shake a bottle of food color without triple-checking the cap. Yet here I am, splattered with red like an extra in a slasher movie. This couldn't have happened on a worse day.

"Shit," I curse, looking for somewhere to drop the dripping bottle without causing more carnage. It's no easy feat: almost thirty years as a baker, and I still work like a tornado. I like to do a big cleanup at the end of the day, the repetition of it helping me switch off. Which is fine, until I'm in a rush in the middle of my workday and can't find an empty spot.

Eventually, I just drop the bottle in the sink and wince as color splatters up the sides. I quickly strip off my apron and wash my hands before hurrying to my supply shelves in search of a new bottle of cherry red.

I scan the shelves: maroon, burgundy, coral. Every damn shade of pink. But no cherry red. I leave the kitchen to check out front, in the café portion of my patisserie. When it's quiet, Gracie, who covers the café side of things, sometimes mixes up frosting behind the counter for me.

She's wiping down the inside of the window as I check her stash. No cherry red. It's a popular color in Wintermore, and I go through it like water. Only in a Christmas-obsessed town like this would an eleven-year-old request a Santa-themed cake for her birthday in September.

None of the other reds I have will do, and there's nothing I can mix to get the perfect shade to match the rest of the cake. A quick glance at my phone confirms that I won't have enough time to get to the kitchen supply store in Jackson before it closes, and this cake is being picked up first thing tomorrow morning.

In other words, I'm screwed. Unless… I peer through the gleaming window, my gaze landing on the bakery across the street. The Enchanted Bakery is bustling with customers.

The family of the owner, Noelle Whitten, is Christmas royalty in this town. There's no way she doesn't keep cherry red on hand. Unfortunately, for reasons I've yet to figure out, Noelle despises me. I've tried to mend whatever bridge I've apparently burned, and I always try to talk to her when we cross paths, but nothing seems to change her feelings toward me. And only me. As far as I can tell, Noelle is a ray of sunshine to everyone else in Wintermore.

"Gracie, would you mind going over to The Enchanted Bakery and asking if they have a bottle of cherry red food color we can borrow? I can replace it in a couple of days."

"No can do," Gracie replies, wrinkling her nose. "My ex-boyfriend's new girlfriend just started working there. Remember?"

Right. Nothing could have prepared me for the amount of drama I'd learn about from hiring a twenty-year-old. I'm only forty-six, but Gracie makes me feel ancient.

"But aren't you dating her ex-boyfriend now? Surely it all cancels each other out."

"It doesn't work like that," she says, like it's the most obvious thing in the world.

I bite my tongue and check the clock above the counter. I have a little over fifteen minutes until my meeting, which gives me just enough time to stop in across the street on the way.

"I'm heading out. I should be back in an hour, two tops," I say, grabbing my denim jacket from the hook as I rush out the door, skipping across the street and tugging it on.

Most people would call me crazy for preferring Wyoming's all-over-the-place weather to sunny California, but I like seeing the passage of time in the turn of the leaves. Things fall apart, people die, and dreams fade into nothing, but the world keeps turning and the seasons keep changing. It's comforting.

Although The Enchanted Bakery is technically a Christmas-themed bakery, Noelle has done an amazing job of making it not feel overwhelming. There are pine boughs, holly, mistletoe, twinkling lights, and pinecones everywhere, and the place smells like apples and cinnamon, but it all comes together tastefully.

To say it's taken off since she opened last year—on Christmas Eve, of course—would be an understatement. I've had a steady stream of customers since opening *Épices et Sucré*, but the bulk of my business comes from orders for special occasion cakes. I'd bet money that Noelle makes just as much from her café as she does from her bakery orders.

From the second she opens the door to the second she locks it, the place is packed. It's busy enough that I have to take a deep breath, focusing on the gaps between customers as I weave my way to the front. I swear she could quadruple the size of the café and still not have enough space for everyone who wants to eat in.

I hover by the end of the counter for a moment until someone comes close enough for me to speak to them.

"Hey. Bryce, right?"

Gracie's ex's new girlfriend raises a brow. "Yeah."

"Shay Harland. I own *Épices et Sucré* across the street."

Recognition dawns on her face, but she doesn't speak any further, so I continue.

"I was hoping you might have a bottle of cherry red Mira-Color food color I could borrow."

Bryce shrugs. "I don't know."

For the love of god. "Is there someone I could ask that might know?"

She points over her shoulder at a door. "You can go back."

"Thanks."

The kitchen door is framed with a garland of baubles, and there's a kitschy "Santa's Elves Only!" sign that looks hand-painted. It's cute.

I push the door open and swallow at the sight of the bustling kitchen. It's a world away from my quiet kitchen across the street —but somehow more organized, considering there are at least five people working in here.

No one looks up as I close the door behind me. I recognize the level of focus in the eyes of the woman piping macarons closest to the door, and I know better than to interrupt.

I peer around, looking for someone who doesn't look like they're in the middle of something, but there's only one person not actively mixing, decorating, or slicing.

Noelle is standing in the back corner, flicking through some kind of paperwork. She's not who I would have chosen to ask, but she's my best option, so I carefully move across the kitchen and stop in front of her.

She looks up, confusion that's quickly replaced by annoyance, flickering on her face.

"Hi!" I say brightly, but that just seems to piss her off more. "Bryce said I could come back."

Noelle looks over my shoulder at the door, her lips in a thin line, and something tells me Bryce isn't going to be in her good books.

"Can I help you?" she says without looking back at me.

I don't know how old she is, but Noelle is a lot younger than me. Yet, somehow, she makes me feel like I'm about to be scolded by a teacher or something. I'm not sure where her family is from, but her dad and uncle both have thick southern drawls. Noelle's accent is deep and rich, with only a little twang now and again.

"I was wondering if you had a bottle of MiraColor cherry red I could borrow? I'll replace it, but I spilled my last bottle, and I need it to finish a custom cake, and I have a meeting, so I can't get to Jackson and I—" I close my mouth as Noelle turns away from me, stalking across the floor toward the cabinets lining the side of the kitchen.

She's tall, but she still has to stand on her tiptoes to rummage around the top shelf. I take her in, dragging my eyes up the long line of her body.

In the years I've lived in Wintermore, Noelle must have had hair every color of the rainbow, but right now it's a pretty purple. It makes her blue eyes pop, and her rosy cheeks somehow pinker. She's beautiful all year, but I've noticed the change in her as the leaves have turned.

It's clear she's exhausted—there are smudges under her eyes and every bone in her body seems tense—but I see her in the morning when she steps outside and breathes in the crisp fall air. I've seen how her eyes sparkle, how, for a moment, it doesn't seem like the weight of the world is on her shoulders.

"Here you go." She turns and thrusts a brand-new bottle of cherry red into my hand. Thank god.

"Thank you so much. You're a lifesaver, seriously. I'll replace it as soon as my order comes—"

"Don't worry about it," she says, quickly cutting me off. She clears her throat, crossing her arms. "I actually have to run. I have a meeting at The Frosty Bean."

It's clear she wants me to leave. I'm not ignorant of the fact that she doesn't like being around me. Which is why it makes no sense for me to open my mouth and reply, "I do too! Let's walk over together."

Noelle isn't an asshole. She doesn't like me, I know that, but she's never overtly impolite. Just a little short with me. I can't imagine her being rude, but, for a moment, I can tell she wants to be.

The polite thing for me to do would be to make up an excuse to run back across the street, but Noelle closes her eyes and sighs before I get the chance.

"Sure. Let's."

I swear I can hear her gritted teeth.

She calls goodbye and leads me out the back door into a little courtyard area with trash cans, a pile of broken-down cardboard boxes, and a small shelter with chopped logs. I've seen the smoke coiling from the chimney in her apartment, and I've spent many cold nights a little jealous. The virtual fireplace I put on my TV sometimes doesn't hit the same as a real one.

Noelle cuts around the side of the building and through the tight alleyway, leading us back to the main street.

"Why don't you just go through the café?" I ask as she crosses her arms across her chest. Surely it would be faster.

"Whenever I step foot in the café, everyone wants to talk to me. To ask about my family, the toy store, if I have a girlfriend yet. Small-town shit," she says with a shrug.

I didn't grow up in a town like Wintermore, but I've been here long enough to witness what she's talking about. This town isn't unfriendly to tourists, but the locals stick together and do everything they can to support each other. Noelle is Wintermore's darling, and I'm not surprised everyone is so excited to support her.

Wintermore is laid out kind of like a tree. Main Street is the trunk, with the bulk of the town's businesses lining each side. Most people live on the little streets that branch off Main Street, but there are a few houses and businesses dotted around up toward the mountain, where the trees are thick enough that it's practically a forest. My favorite part of town is the river, and the reservoir it leads to if you follow it far enough. There's not a spot in Wintermore that doesn't have a view of the mountains, but the view from the reservoir is unmatched. I've spent hours sitting by the water, staring up at the towering hills.

My brother lives in the mountains. It's not far, but the drive is treacherous, and I'm not a confident driver on the easiest of roads, so I don't make it up as often as I should, considering I moved out here to be close to him. But there's something about surrounding myself with trees and looking up at the mountains that makes me feel more connected to him.

"Who are you meeting at The Frosty Bean? A customer?" I ask. I'm being nosy, I know, but I've never been good at awkward silences.

Noelle sucks in a breath before answering. "I have a meeting with the mayor."

Huh. But I…

"Mayor Blackwood?"

"That's the one," she confirms, and I appreciate her not calling me on what a stupid question it is. Of course there's only one mayor.

"My meeting is with her," I say, and Noelle looks over at me, her eyes narrowed. "Did she tell you what it was about?"

"Nope, just that she needed to talk to me about something."

"Same."

I assumed that Mayor Blackwood wanted to order a cake or something for one of the many events she throws. I have no idea what she could want with both Noelle and me, unless she's planning an event big enough for two bakers. We'll find out soon, I guess.

It only takes us a few minutes to walk to The Frosty Bean, and Noelle holds the door open for me, letting me in first. We take a seat in a booth with a window view, crispy red and orange leaves brushing the glass.

"Hey, you two." Bianca, the owner of The Frosty Bean, is surprised to see us together and doesn't bother to hide it. She arches a brow, flicking her gaze between the two of us. "What can I get for you?"

I gesture for Noelle to order first, and she purses her lips, like she's pissed at the politeness.

"I'll do a gingerbread latte, extra cinnamon, please."

"And a hazelnut mocha for me—extra cream," I say. Bianca scribbles down our orders.

"Just a heads up, Mayor Blackwood is joining us," Noelle chimes in, and Bianca's face falls.

"Ugh. Thanks for the warning. I'll have your drinks out in a sec."

I'm not familiar with the mayor, but that reaction doesn't fill me with confidence. "I don't know Mayor Blackwood—should I be worried?" I ask Noelle, and she shrugs.

"She's fine, just intense. And she's not my biggest fan."

It's not like Noelle to be forthcoming with anything personal —not to me, anyway—and I pounce on it.

"How come?"

Noelle seems to realize she's made a misstep, and it's possible I sound a little too enthusiastic about having an *in*. I can't help it; I want Noelle to like me. She seems so fun, and her baking is amazing. Wintermore is friendly, if a little distant, with newcomers, and I don't have any real friends here. So, naturally, the one friend I'd like is the one person who seems to actively dislike me.

"I dated her daughter in high school," Noelle answers, crossing her arms. "It didn't end badly or anything—we just went to different colleges and drifted apart—but I don't think Mayor Blackwood was ever really on board with her daughter dating a woman. Also, everyone wanted my mom to run for mayor, and the only reason Mayor Blackwood won is because my mom didn't run."

"I would've voted for your mom," I say, and she hums her agreement.

"Everyone would've voted for my mom."

Noelle's parents are the best of Wintermore—kind and welcoming, Christmas-obsessed, and their family toy store is a huge boost to the town's economy.

Bianca drops our drinks off, and I check the time on my phone.

"She's always late," Noelle says, of the mayor. "But god forbid you're ever late to see her."

Excellent. I love sitting here trying to find something to talk about with someone who doesn't want to talk to me.

Noelle is silent, toying with a sugar packet, looking everywhere but at me. It takes everything in me not to fill the silence.

I grew up in a loud house. I'm a triplet, and my mom ran a daycare, so it was never quiet. It was happy and busy and chaotic. Until it wasn't, and silence reminds me of *after*, so I do my best to avoid it. When I'm working alone in the kitchen, I always have something on—music, a podcast, an audiobook, The Food Network.

"Do you—" I begin, but Noelle interrupts me.

"My niece swiped yes on you on Locked."

It takes me a second to process what she's said. "Locked... the dating app? Isn't your niece a baby?"

"Yes. She grabbed my phone," Noelle replies. "Rora—you know Rora, right?" I nod. "She signed me up for the app, and your profile was the first to show up. Sunny grabbed for my phone and, you know."

It's clear that Noelle would not have swiped yes, and I wouldn't expect her to. I have to be a good fifteen years older than her, and she hates me.

"Honestly, I wouldn't have noticed. I haven't opened Locked in years. I don't even know if I still have the app downloaded."

Noelle leans forward a fraction, like I've piqued her interest.

"Why? Is there something wrong with it?"

"Not really. It's just mostly tourists, and I don't think I'm a casual dating person."

"You don't think?" Noelle asks, and while I don't particularly want to get into my dating history, this is the most interested she's ever seemed in me.

"I got divorced just before I moved here, and I haven't really tried dating since. Definitely nothing casual. Maybe I'd like it, but I don't know… Who has the time?" I've struck a decent work-life balance since opening the patisserie, but I value my free time too much to spend it pretending to be interested in strangers and exchanging mediocre orgasms. Maybe that's cynical of me, but I haven't had truly good sex since college.

My ex-husband tried, but now that we're on the other side of things, I can admit to myself that I was never actually attracted to him. I married him because my family needed something good after so much bad, and he was a good friend. We were both relieved to go our separate ways.

Noelle rolls her neck, her eyes closed, and my gaze snags on the dips of her collarbone. I swallow, my cheeks warming.

"Who has the time, indeed," she says, and this might be the first time she's ever willingly agreed on anything with me. "But dating is more of a time commitment than a casual hookup. Not that I have enough time for either, these days."

Her lips lift in a wry smile as she opens her eyes, and I swallow, my cheeks warming.

"Anyway," she continues. "All of that to say, if you re-download the app, it was Sunny. Not me."

And just like that, her smile is gone, and frosty Noelle is back.

I open my mouth to reply, but the loud clip-clop of heels sounds on the café's hardwood floors, and we both turn to see the mayor. She smiles widely at the sight of us.

"Excellent. You're both here. Let's get started."

3
NOELLE

I t's a fundamental rule of staying in your hometown that the people who watched you grow up will never truly see you as an adult. Even Rora, who's a mom herself, still has people telling her how tall she's gotten when they haven't seen her in a while—a bold-faced lie, considering she's not even five feet.

I'm thirty years old, and Angela Blackwood still treats me like the teenager who *corrupted* her perfect daughter.

"Please, call me Angela," she tells Shay as they shake hands, mere seconds after I greeted her as Mayor Blackwood and she said nothing of the sort.

"Shuffle along, Noelle," Mayor Blackwood says, flicking her hand in my direction.

I grit my teeth and slide over on the bench so she can sit beside me.

Shay narrows her soft gray eyes, glancing between me and the mayor, the dismissiveness not escaping her notice.

I've been dreading this meeting since Mayor Blackwood called yesterday. We've never seen eye to eye, and I do my best to avoid her. Shay showing up in my kitchen when I was already in a shitty mood really was the icing on top of the cake. But she was frazzled—spilling your last bottle of red food color in a Christmas town will do that to you—and it's so rare to see her shaken, that it knocked me off my axis.

I know very little about Shay, other than she moved here a few years ago to be close to her brother, who lives in a cabin on the mountain, she's a baker, she's into women, and she's divorced—the last two are recent revelations. It's not like I've ever had much of a reason to pay attention to her over her business. I'd guess she's somewhere in her early to mid-forties, given the fine crinkles around her gray eyes and the smile lines that frame her face. She has long blonde hair that she sometimes wears in a French braid when she's baking, fine pink lips, and very white and straight teeth. She always wears a gold heart-shaped locket with a swirly G on it, and she toys with it constantly.

If the Wintermore whispers are anything to go by, she could be from California, New York, Michigan, or Colorado. California would be my guess, if the rumor mill is correct, but the rumor mill is rarely the most accurate source of information. I once heard through the grapevine that my parents were getting a divorce because someone supposedly heard them arguing over which kind of peanut butter to buy at the grocery store. Mom's a crunchy person, Dad's a smooth guy, but it's all a moot point, because Felix and I are both allergic.

I grab for my latte and take a sip just as she says, "So, Mayor Blackwood—" and almost spit it out.

For a brief moment, I actually like her. It's gone as soon as I feel it, though.

"What is it you wanted to talk to me and Noelle about?" Shay asks, and I appreciate her not beating around the bush.

Mayor Blackwood looks mildly affronted, but she shakes it off quickly. "Well, we have an exciting opportunity that I think would be beneficial for both our town and our residents, but I need your help to make it happen. Both of you. Shay, are you familiar with *A Christmas Wish in the Mountains*?"

Shay nods, and I'm not surprised. You'd be hard-pressed to find anyone in Wintermore who doesn't know the movie that made us famous like the back of their hand.

"Excellent," the mayor says, clapping her hands. "As I'm sure you both know, the tourism the movie brings us is vital to this town, but it has dwindled over the past couple of years. The more Christmas movies that release, the less relevant we become."

We first noticed the drop in the run-up to Christmas last year. My brother did, anyway. The Enchanted Workshop usually sees a spike in sales from September, but it was a slow start last year. But, in an unusual move from Felix, he had a good idea and started pushing the online store. He hired his best friend's sister, Abigail, to run the online side of things and push the store on social media, and profits actually increased last holiday season—and they've stayed steady since. And, of course, my bakery has been as busy as the day it opened.

From what I've heard, the rest of the town hasn't been so lucky.

"I've been in contact with the network," Mayor Blackwood continues. "I asked if they'd be interested in filming some kind of sequel here, and we've been in talks over the past few months, but I wasn't expecting anything to happen for years. However…" She leans in, beckoning us closer and lowering her voice, like she's sharing a secret. "They were supposed to film a fall movie up in Maine this year, but the town flooded. So they're pivoting. They've pulled together a script that works as a sequel, with the actors they have, and want to film a fall movie here, to release next year."

I narrow my eyes. "A fall movie in a Christmas town?"

The idea sounds stupid, but I can't deny that it might be nice to spread the busy season out a little. We get an influx every Christmas, and the truly Christmas-obsessed folks visit year-round, but, for the most part, the rest of the year is pretty normal for a small mountain town in Wyoming.

It wouldn't be the worst thing to have another season in Wintermore's pocket—I suppose not everyone is as obsessed with Christmas as we are.

But a new movie being filmed doesn't explain why I'm squeezed into a booth with Shay and Mayor Blackwood.

"What does this have to do with us?" Shay asks the question that's already playing on my mind.

"The movie follows the daughter of the couple from the first movie, all grown-up, and her old high school nemesis, owning rival bakeries. There's some kind of competition involved. You know what these movies are like," the mayor says, waving a hand dismissively. "They want to use your bakeries, and—"

"For how long?" I interrupt, ignoring Mayor Blackwood's scandalized expression at my rudeness. "We can't just close our bakeries."

"I'm not sure of the logistics, but you would be well compensated, and we can find a space for the two of you to work. Don't you have a kitchen in your basement, Noelle?"

I do, but there's no way I could fit Shay and my whole team in there. At least she only has Gracie working with her, but I have seven employees.

"So we'd work… together?" Shay asks.

"Exactly. And they want you to bake together, too!"

Mayor Blackwood seems excited, but that sounds like a lot more than just letting them use our bakeries.

"How much work would this entail?" I ask because I need more details before I can make any promises.

"Well, the network wants to source as much as they can from Wintermore—it's a good marketing point—so they want the two of you to work together to bake for the movie. As I said, you'll be well compensated."

I almost laugh. Where am I supposed to pull the extra pair of hands and hours in a day from?

It sounds like a whole lot of extra work I have neither the time nor space for. Not to mention the fact that I'm already sacrificing sleep to try and fit everything into my day.

As if she can see the thoughts rattling around my brain, Mayor Blackwood adds, "I don't know exactly how much work it would be. The network is sending people, and they can explain everything. But what I do know is that this would be great for all of us. For the town, for you, for your bakeries—think of the marketing! And you'll be credited in the movies. I don't see any downsides, personally."

"When would this be happening?" Shay asks. Shit, that should've been my first question.

"They're looking to start filming in ten days, but they'll be in town at the start of next week, so they'll want to meet with you then."

She has to be fucking kidding me. "Ten days? Are you serious?"

"It's a last-minute project!" she protests. "They need to film this fall to release next fall. We're lucky they could squeeze us in."

"It's not exactly a lot of notice for us to figure things out with our schedules and clients," Shay points out, and I find myself agreeing with her. What the hell is happening?

The mayor frowns, like she expected Shay, at least, would be on her side. "It's short notice, I'll give you that. But the network is being very accommodating. They'll pay for extra staff if you need help with your existing work, and they're going to be building temporary workspaces for anyone displaced during filming, so if you need more space, we can make that happen. I think this could be good for everyone."

Shay presses her lips together in a thin line, and it looks like she's seriously considering this. I know her patisserie isn't as busy as The Enchanted Bakery, but even she has to know how ridiculous this is.

I drain the last of my latte, scrunching my nose at the pool of syrup at the bottom. Pushing my cup away, I lean back against the booth and turn to the mayor.

"Look, while I appreciate the idea and I don't think it would be a bad thing to bring more tourism to town, it's just not feasible for me to do something like this on such short notice. The bakery is so busy, and I—"

"And who do you owe that business to, Noelle?" Mayor Blackwood says, folding her arms across her chest.

"I'm sorry?"

"You wouldn't be in Wintermore if it weren't for the Christmas movie. Your family wouldn't have the toy store, and you wouldn't have your bakery—your niece wouldn't exist. This town has given and given and given to you and your family. They've supported you since day one, and I would think you'd want to support them back."

Her words curdle my stomach, stretching the tension I hold there so tight it's a wonder it doesn't snap.

"Hey now, that's not necess—"

"Fine," I answer, interrupting Shay. I don't need her coming to my defense. Not when Mayor Blackwood is right.

This town has given me everything, the goddamn movie has given me everything. My family has thrived here: we met Rora, and Rora met Uncle Henry; our toy store has been more than successful; my bakery is killing it. All of my dreams have come true.

What kind of person gets everything they ever wanted and hates every second of it?

An ungrateful brat who can't handle a little hard work, apparently.

"I'll do it." I look up at Shay, and she's watching me with an expression I don't recognize. "Are you in?"

Shay side eyes the mayor for a second before focusing back on me. "Are you sure? If it's too much—"

"I said I'd do it, Shay." I'm not proud of my tone, or the flash of disappointment that flicks through Shay's eyes.

She nods. "Alright. I'm in."

4

SHAY

I don't know Noelle Whitten well, but I know she's not okay. The mayor was out of line, trying, and succeeding, to guilt Noelle into something she clearly doesn't want to do.

A thick silence stretches between us as we walk down the street. I understand Noelle's hesitance toward the project—it's a lot of work, and ridiculously last-minute. But I'm still excited.

The money alone will be great, but the exposure will be invaluable. And I think it'll be fun to see how a movie is made.

As for working so closely with Noelle… maybe this is what we need to find common ground. Maybe I'll figure out why Noelle doesn't like me when we're shoved in a kitchen together, and maybe she'll realize I'm not so bad.

Maybe we could actually become friends.

Unlike now, when I can sense the dislike emanating from her. I'm sure the last thing she wants is to talk to me, but I can't see the tension weighing down her spine and *not* say something.

"Are you okay?"

Noelle doesn't even look up. "I'm fine."

"It just seems like you don't want to do this, and I'm sure it's not too late to—"

She stops and whirls around, her lilac hair flying. "I said I'm fine, and I said I'd do it."

"Okay. But you seem stressed about it, and we are going to be working together, so you're going to have to be okay with me checking in," I answer gently.

Noelle narrows her eyes. "You don't have to check in. We're temporarily working together. We're not friends."

Ouch.

The sensible thing would be to ask her why she doesn't like me, or we're going to spend the next few weeks tiptoeing around it. But I can't imagine she'd respond well to me asking right now.

"Right. Well, as temporary colleagues, we should probably talk about how we're going to work together. Do you want to come over and we can figure things out?"

"Fine," Noelle replies through gritted teeth.

She follows me across the street and into *Épices et Sucré*. A couple I don't recognize is sitting at the round table by the window, and we greet each other before Noelle and I take a seat on the other side of the café.

"Can I get you anything?"

"I'm fine," Noelle answers—her favorite response, apparently—but her stomach rumbles. She glares down at it.

"Did you eat lunch? You seemed busy earlier."

"I'll get something later."

I sigh and turn to call to Gracie, "Can you put together a couple of plates of the afternoon tea stuff in the back fridge?"

We don't generally serve savory food, but our afternoon teas are popular. I always prep a few savories in the morning, and Gracie and I eat any leftovers. I can't remember the last time I had to make lunch. Although I opened *Épices et Sucré* with the intention of running a real French patisserie, Wintermore has more of a taste for gingerbread than millefeuille. Now, we do a little of everything. It's not a good business model, and I've been thinking about rebranding for years, but I've never gotten around to it. The money from the movie might be the push I need.

"I don't suppose there's any point in me saying no," Noelle says, crossing her arms.

"Correct. Obviously, you don't really want to do this."

"It's not that I don't want to do it, it's that I don't know how I'm supposed to find the time," Noelle corrects. "I'm already busier than I can handle."

"You know, I'd be happy to help if—"

"I don't need your help," she snaps. "Why do you care so much about this?" Noelle asks. "The movie means a lot to my family, but you have no obligation here."

I glance around the café. "I'm not struggling, but I want to change things up a little, and this would help. Besides, the movie means a lot to my family, too. It was my sister's favorite."

Noelle tilts her head. "You have a sister?"

I rub my locket with my thumb. This part never gets easier. It's been two decades, and it still cleaves me in two to open my mouth and reply, "Had. Georgie. She died before she got the chance to come to Wintermore."

Noelle's sky-blue eyes widen. She's a sister; she's probably imagining what it would be like to wake up in a world without Felix or Rora. I used to do the same whenever I heard that people had lost siblings. But nothing prepared me for what it was actually like.

Georgie, Nico, and I were triplets—*are* triplets. Three whole people, but also three parts of something bigger. Now, I have to fight to even feel like one whole person. Nico stopped fighting a long time ago.

"I'm so sorry," Noelle says. I'm used to the sentiment, but usually it's awkward and hurried, like whoever has stumbled onto this darker point of my life can't wait to get away from it. Not Noelle. "Is that why you moved here? To honor Georgie?"

Hearing my sister's name on her lips is like an electric shock. For some reason, people avoid calling her by her name, even my parents and Nico. Sometimes, I find myself just saying it out loud when I'm alone because it's been so long since anyone has, and I refuse to forget how it feels to form her name.

"Kind of, yeah. My brother Nico moved here after she died—he lives on the mountain, and he doesn't come down often. I thought if I moved here after my divorce, that it might help him, I don't know, be less of a recluse? No luck on that front," I say with a wry smile and a shrug. "He's frustrating as hell, but he's my brother, so I'll keep trying."

"I understand frustrating brothers," Noelle offers, as Gracie comes over and sets two plates of food and a jug of peach lemonade on the table.

I use the distraction to steer us toward a lighter topic. "How do you want to try and divide up work? I can close without much trouble—I have a few custom orders a week, but I can work on them anywhere. I'm guessing closing would be a lot more complicated for you." Gracie can handle the admin stuff she usually does from home, and I can give her paid time off for the rest of her hours. Noelle has a full staff, not to mention lines out the door most days.

"It would." Noelle sighs and picks at a cucumber stick. At first, I think she's taking the skin off because she doesn't like it—exactly like I do—but she pops the skin in her mouth and leaves the rest. Weird. "There's plenty of space in my basement kitchen for you to work on your custom orders, and for us to work on stuff for the movie, but I can't fit my team down there, and, even if we did close the café for a month—which, realistically, I can't—we have mail pre-orders and a lot of local orders."

"I can't imagine they're going to have to spend a month straight in either of our places, so hopefully the network people will have a plan for that," I offer, but she just chews her lip.

"I think it makes sense that we spend the mornings working on our own bakery stuff, and then I can come down to the basement after lunch and we can work on movie stuff. Assuming that works with whatever they want us to do."

It makes sense, but my skin prickles at the thought of working in a basement. "Are there windows in your basement?" I ask, and Noelle's gaze falls to my fingers, and the hummus sandwich I'm squeezing tightly between them. I put the sandwich down.

"There are a couple of small windows and a door. It's meant for loading and unloading, I think. I don't really use it, but you can open it if you need to."

I breathe a sigh of relief. "That's good. Thanks."

She says nothing, just searches my face until I explain. "I'm claustrophobic. I can manage most days, but some days are worse than others, so it helps me to be prepared."

"You can come over and check it out whenever you want. If it doesn't work, we'll figure something else out." Noelle says it matter-of-factly, like it's no big deal.

For a moment, it feels like I'm seeing the same Noelle the rest of Wintermore does—maybe not as soft and sunshiney, but certainly less prickly than I usually get.

"Is there anything I need to know about working with you?"

She considers for a moment before saying, "I'm allergic to peanuts and pistachios."

"Airborne?"

"As far as I know. A lot of people grow out of airborne allergies, and I haven't checked since I was a kid. It doesn't seem worth the risk."

Working in the culinary world with any kind of allergy is frustrating, but I don't think I'd risk it, either.

"I don't work with a lot of peanuts or pistachios, but I'll make sure I have none around when we're working together," I promise. "Are almonds okay? I use a lot of them."

"Almonds are fine. You know, I honestly don't know how this is going to work. We work on completely different things."

Does she think having a patisserie means I can't bake? Granted, I don't get the chance nearly as often as I'd like these days, but baking is where I started.

My siblings and I all grew up with a creative outlet. For Nico, it was wood—processing, carving, building. For me, it was baking. I spent every free moment in the kitchen, baking up a storm. I had more fails than wins in my younger days, but I loved it.

Georgie was always less creative than Nico and me, but she loved art. For as long as I can remember, she was obsessed with Paris—the galleries, the fashion, the patisseries.

As teenagers, we dreamed together of opening a patisserie. I'd run the kitchen; she'd run everything else. Now, I'm following our dream without her.

"I've worked in plenty of bakeries over the years," I assure Noelle. "I'll be fine with whatever they throw at us."

Noelle doesn't look convinced, but she nods, anyway. She eyes the cookies and cream brownie on her plate before grabbing it and gingerly nibbling a corner. Her eyes widen, and she takes a bigger bite.

"Shit. That's good," she murmurs, sounding surprisingly pissed off about it.

She pushes her plate away and stands. "Well, I suppose we'll just have to wait and see what the network has in mind for us. I'll see you when they want to meet with us, I guess."

I don't even get the chance to respond before she's running out the door, like she reached her limit and can't bear to spend another second in my presence.

Maybe not friends, then.

5
NOELLE

There's something about seeing my whole family crowded around my parents' kitchen table. It's the same one we've had since we moved to Wintermore, and so many memories have been made here.

Rora's first Whitten family dinner, when she was seven and I was eight, and we already knew we were meant to find each other.

Celebratory hot chocolate after surviving our first holiday season in The Enchanted Workshop.

Being surrounded by glitter and markers, making signs when Felix and his best friend, Quinn, decided to try football one year —and hated it.

Me and Rora staying up past midnight the day after we found out we would be hundreds of miles apart for college.

Rora and Uncle Henry telling us they were having a baby.

I love it here. This town, this home, this family.

Between the movie, the café, and Shay goddamn Harland, everything feels a little out of whack right now, but being here helps.

Of course, the movie is everyone's favorite topic of conversation tonight.

A Christmas Wish in the Mountains is, to this day, my parents' favorite movie. It's not that the movie itself is any good—though, by made-for-TV Christmas movie standards, it's not bad—but what it did for our family. My dad says the moment he saw Wintermore on our old box TV, he knew that was where the Whitten family was meant to be. And he was right.

Needless to say, he and my mom are excited about the new movie. Technically, it's a secret, for now, which means the whole town is pretending they don't know about it.

"Doesn't it feel like kismet?" my dad asks, rubbing the top of my head as he passes the table on his way to the fridge. "Our family toy store appearing in the very movie franchise that made us open it!"

"I don't think you can call it a movie franchise with two movies, Dad," Felix points out, but my dad is too happy to pay him any mind.

Felix didn't protest The Enchanted Workshop's involvement in the movie:

"Abigail says it'll be great for social media," he told us, and I know right away that meant he'd agreed. Whatever Abigail says goes in The Enchanted Workshop these days. As it should—Felix made the best decision he's ever made in hiring his best friend's sister. She has a knack for business that makes me wonder how nobody noticed it earlier.

"What do you think about all of this?" I ask Rora. She's been awfully quiet, considering how much she loathes *A Christmas Wish in the Mountains*, and what it did to her hometown.

Unlike my parents, Rora's settled in Wintermore long before the movie was even thought of because they were photographers looking for a quiet, scenic place to raise their daughter. Seven years and one movie later, Wintermore was so full of tourists that they couldn't work here anymore. The pressure of it all destroyed their marriage and made Rora hate all things Christmas.

Her parents are back together now, and I (unfortunately) know that she has a thing for my uncle Henry when he's dressed up as

Santa, so I assume she's mostly over it. Still, her nose wrinkles at the question.

"I don't know," she says, stroking Sunny's cheek where it rests on my uncle Henry's shoulder. "It kind of messes with our plans a little. We were hoping to stick around town for a while longer than we originally planned, but if it's going to be as busy as it was when we were kids… It's just not how I want our kids to grow up."

I don't miss the plural "kids," and neither does my mom, if the smile she hides behind her hand is anything to go by. She knows better than to comment, but anyone with eyes could see how much they love being parents, and I'd be surprised if Rora wasn't pregnant again before Sunny's first birthday.

Wintermore was a great place to grow up, for nine months of the year. It was busy, sure, but manageable. November through January, though… Main Street was like Times Square every day for three months straight. I love people, and I love Christmas, but even I remember the relief of days we didn't have to leave the house.

I don't want kids of my own, but I see Rora's point.

"Word on the street is that you're going to be working with Shay Harland," my mom says.

I roll my eyes. Secrets in small towns, I swear to god. Shay probably told Gracie, who probably told her boyfriend, who probably told his mom, and so on and so forth. I don't know where Shay's from originally, but she's probably not used to the small-town rumor mill. She's been here for a few years, but, as far as I can tell, she isn't close to anyone in town.

She earned every bit of success her patisserie has had. The town didn't show up and just hand it to her.

"Yeah, I am. They want to film in both of our places, and Shay and I are going to be baking the stuff for the baking competition in the movie."

Rora's eyebrows practically reach her hairline. "Together?"

Even Sunny has an expression of disbelief.

"Together," I confirm. "Trust me, I'm as unhappy about it as you might expect."

"I don't know why you can't just get along, Noelle," my mom scolds me. "Shay's a sweetheart, and there's plenty of space in this town for both of you."

"We get along fine. I don't have to be her bestie."

I'm well aware that "get along" is an exaggeration, and all of the effort has been on Shay's side. My mom isn't wrong; there's enough space in Wintermore for both of our businesses to thrive. Hell, at this point, I reckon there could be a whole street of bakeries, and we'd all manage just fine. Wintermorons (the official term, for some godforsaken reason) love their treats.

But it's not about Shay starting her business first. Not anymore. It's about the easy smile on her face when I see her walking out of *Épices et Sucré* every night. It's about the weight of the world that's on my shoulders, not hers.

Needless to say, I'm grown enough to know it's not about Shay. But that doesn't mean I have to like her.

"You could say no," Uncle Henry suggests, bouncing a cooing Sunny. "You shouldn't have to do it if you don't want to."

"You'd think, but apparently I have an obligation to Wintermore after all it's done for me."

My mom narrows her eyes. "Is that what Angela Blackwood told you?"

"It's fine, Mom. I've already agreed, and she has a point. I'll always be grateful to the movie for bringing us here, and I should do my part."

My family doesn't look convinced, but the last thing I want to do is worry them. I try my best not to show how much I'm struggling with the weight of everything, and how much the pressure of our family name has been more of a burden than a blessing this past year.

I am grateful, that part isn't a lie. I'm just stretched too thin. And I know if my family knew how much I was struggling with everything, they wouldn't hesitate to jump in and help—just like I know that I could probably stand to outsource a chunk of my work, and set some boundaries with the townsfolk, so I could actually get in the kitchen again.

This is everything I've ever wanted, and I can't bring myself to give up any responsibility or leave anything to chance.

6

SHAY

My cat, who isn't actually my cat, is waiting by the back door for me when I finally finish up with the last of the dishes.

"Hi, Cat," I say as I crouch down to pick him up, because I don't know his name. I'm not even sure he's a *him*, I just have a feeling.

I don't know much about cats, but I have access to Google, the same as everyone else. After a shit ton of research, I came to the conclusion that he's just a cat. It seems like cats are either ridiculously fancy or just cats. And Cat, as I call him—because I'm so original—falls into the latter category.

He started showing up here a couple of years ago, on Halloween, to be exact. At first, I thought he was a decoration— that seemed more logical than a black cat deciding the potted camellias I keep out front were the perfect bed. I almost shit myself when he started following me up to my apartment.

I asked around to see if anyone was missing him, but no one ever claimed him, and no one recognized him. He doesn't have a microchip, and he didn't have a collar. He's always come and gone as he pleases, but these days, he's here more than he's gone. If he has another home, they must not be too worried about him.

It's been long enough that I should probably name him and

commit to the little creature that seems to have claimed me, but I'm terrified that the second I do, his actual owners will pop up out of the woodwork and I'll be forced to give up the only friend I have in this town.

"How was your day?" I murmur in a baby voice, and Cat meows back as I carry him upstairs to my apartment.

Living above the patisserie is unbelievably convenient, and I love my apartment. It's not big, but it's enough for one person— and a cat who unofficially lives here. There's a cozy bedroom, a big kitchen/living room, and a bathroom with a deep soaking tub, that's exactly what I need after long days in the kitchen. I've been known to spend hours soaking, letting the water skim over my skin long after it's chilled and the bubbles have all gone.

I fall asleep in the bath more often than I'd like to admit, but Cat is usually pretty good at waking me up when he wants more food, which is often.

The best part of the apartment, by far, is the fenced-in terrace that sits on top of the roof of my café below. French doors lead off my living room onto the terrace, where I have outdoor furniture, tons of plants, and a perfect view of Wintermore. It's a sun trap, but there's plenty of shade up against the apartment, and my plants are thriving.

Cat loves to lie on the sun-heated stones, and it's the perfect spot to enjoy my coffee and breakfast before heading downstairs to start my day.

I feed Cat, giving him a scratch between his ears as he purrs his thanks, and open the terrace doors, letting in the cool mountain air. I love the smell of fall—crisp and earthy.

The privacy on my terrace is a little lacking, but I don't mind people being able to see up, since it means I can see down. I can also see across the street to other rooftop terraces and balconies.

Noelle doesn't spend a lot of time in her apartment, let alone on her balcony, but I've seen her sitting out there sometimes in the wee hours of the morning when I can't sleep, pacing back and forth or just staring into space.

She reminds me of me when I was in the last couple of years of my marriage, trying to make sense of my head versus my heart. I don't know what she's toiling over, but I can tell there's something, and I'm guessing she doesn't get a lot of time to switch off, considering how busy she is with work.

Her apartment is dark tonight, save for the Christmas lights that twinkle on her balcony and in her bedroom window year-round.

I was worried that Main Street would be a nightmare to live on, between the highway that cuts right through the center of town and the bars and restaurants that stay open late. But even in Wintermore's busiest season, I find I don't mind the noise, the chaos. The quiet days are harder, and tonight is particularly quiet.

I head back into the apartment to grab my phone, a glass of white wine, and leftover spring rolls from my fridge, before sinking into the Papasan chair on the terrace.

Pulling up my message thread with Nico, I type out a quick text:

Hey. All good with you?

Everything's fine. You?

Same. Have you called Mom and Dad recently?

Last week. They seem fine.

Great! I'll call them tomorrow and check in.

Nico doesn't reply, and I sigh, chewing my lip. Like pulling blood from a stone.

Do you need anything? Food, firewood, etc.?

I work with wood for a living, Shay. If I needed firewood, I think I'd have bigger problems.

But no, thank you. I'm all set.

Business going well?

Nico's childhood woodworking hobby serves him well working at his cabin up on the mountain. He makes furniture by commission. Everything is arranged online and shipped to his customers. He has a bit of a cult following and makes decent money. Besides, it's not like he needs much to get by up there.

I trace the curve of the cherrywood elephant he sent me a few months ago. It sits on my terrace table, but I have tons of little trinkets dotted around my apartment. Every couple of months, the courier who collects his furniture pieces to take them to the delivery warehouse up in Jackson stops by and leaves a present from Nico on my doorstep.

We might not talk as often as I'd like, nor are our conversations particularly in-depth, but this is his way of letting me know he's thinking of me. I treasure each and every one.

Business is good. Working on a headboard.

He attaches a picture of the intricately carved wooden headboard. It's only half finished, but it's already gorgeous.

Looks amazing!

Let me know if you need anything, yeah?

Yeah.

Love you, Shay.

Love you. I'll come see you soon.

I close the thread, lean my head back, and sigh at the stars. There are a million little stars shining over Wintermore, and I swear I've wished on every one at some point for my brother back. I think they're ignoring me.

The wine is exactly what I need after my conversation with Nico. I scroll mindlessly through my phone—doom scrolling, Gracie calls it.

I'm not big on social media personally, though I make a lot of content for *Épices et Sucré*'s social media pages. Mostly video montages or slideshows to trending music. One of the first pieces of advice I found when looking up marketing advice was "film everything," and it's easy to just set a tripod up with my old phone and spend a little while each night combing through footage and splicing it together.

I don't post on my personal pages often, but I like seeing what everyone else is doing.

I scroll through Instagram, past cute family pictures from old high school friends I don't talk to anymore, pictures of baking and fancy meals courtesy of my old colleagues and college acquaintances, and ad after ad. I pause on an ad featuring a recognizable bakery counter. Noelle's.

Her Instagram page is gorgeous—it's clear every inch of it has been intentionally curated. Her signature trendy decor style is all over it, but every picture has a festive flair. This seems to piss a lot of people off if the comments are anything to go by:

@suburb4nl3g3nd: Christmas in September, are you kidding me?

@maplesyruplover4: seriously??? wtf

> @cestlabee: some people really do make
> Christmas their whole personality.

But engagement is engagement, and the positive comments far outweigh the negatives.

Besides the Christmassy bakes, she has several saved lives where she just seems to bake in front of the camera, chatting away. Most of them look to be from the early days of her bakery, or before she opened. I imagine she's too busy now.

There are a few more personal pictures scattered throughout, but the one that catches my eye is a picture of Noelle in her Enchanted Bakery apron, holding her niece in a tiny matching apron. It's adorable. Sunny's face is blurred, but Noelle is smiling at her like she's her whole world.

Baby Stanley-Whitten's first day in the kitchen today! I wonder what we'll make…

Rora and Henry are both tagged in the picture, but so is Noelle's personal profile. I click on her username, surprised to see her profile isn't private. She posts a lot, from candid pictures in the bakery to aesthetic pictures of her coffee, and so many family photos. Even tonight, she posted a bunch of pictures of what looks like a family dinner: her parents smiling at each other, Felix cuddling a sleeping Sunny as he and Henry clutch game controllers, a selfie of Noelle and Rora, Noelle smiling at the camera, and Rora looking fondly at her best friend.

From the outside, the Whittens look like the happiest family. I often wonder how many of these kinds of pictures are fake on social media, but it's impossible to believe they're not as close as they look.

I scroll back through her profile, past Sunny's being born, the bakery opening, so many Christmases at The Enchanted Workshop. I find a picture of her with two giant gold foil balloons reading "25." February, five years ago, which means… she's thirty. Sixteen years younger than I am, Jesus. I had no idea what I was doing with my life at thirty, and she's kicking ass, running a successful business.

Impressive doesn't even begin to cover it. Noelle Whitten is something else.

I try to swipe out of the picture, but my phone slips. And in trying to stop it from falling… Fuck. I quickly take back my like, hoping like hell she doesn't have notifications turned on so she doesn't see me, someone who she doesn't like, who doesn't follow her, liking a five-year-old picture. That's enough scrolling for me tonight. Except…

Noelle piqued my interest the other day when she mentioned Locked. It's been so long since I've looked at the app, and it would be nice to meet some new people. My only friend is a cat who doesn't even have a real name. The cat in question hops onto my lap and curls up as my finger hovers over the neon lock app icon.

Maybe it is time I tried dating again. It's been almost five years since Philippe and I got divorced. What's the harm in just talking to people?

I'm not looking for Noelle's profile when I open the app—she's far too young for me, and she's made her feelings about me perfectly clear. But I find myself swiping past the first person to pop up, and the second, and the third, until… There she is.

The first picture on her profile is breathtaking. She's mid-laugh, her lilac hair fluttering in the breeze, with a mug of hot chocolate and a mountain of whipped cream in her hand. There's crushed candy cane sprinkled over the top, and a little dot of cream on the tip of her nose.

I almost press my finger against it, but I catch myself. *What the hell am I doing?*

Blowing out a breath, I close the app before I make a monumental mistake. She said Sunny accidentally swiped on my profile, so if I swipe on her—also accidentally, of course—she'll be notified.

And I don't want Noelle Whitten. I *can't* want Noelle Whitten.

7

NOELLE

can be a raging bitch when I want to be. And, unfortunately,
even when I don't want to be.

Like now: sitting beside Shay fucking Harland in a
production trailer, across from three people from the network
whose job titles I've already forgotten. They're all perfectly nice,
they've been surprisingly forthcoming with information, and
they're going to pay us each a small fortune. But I can't seem to
stop myself from snapping at everything they say. And like she's
trying to piss me off, Shay couldn't be nicer to them.

"We're going to be splitting our trailers across the town—the
park, the grocery store parking lot, a bunch of empty fields, et
cetera—so we're not disrupting any one area too much," the
redhead in the middle explains, and I immediately question her on
traffic controls. Environmental concerns. Wildlife. It's like Rora
has taken over my body, and I half expect the words "fuck Christmas" to slip off my tongue at any moment.

They meet my questions with the patience of saints, smiling
the whole damn time. God, I need to get more sleep. Or maybe
Rora's right and I need a good orgasm or two to de-stress. Clearly,
I'm not taking good enough care of myself.

I jump as Shay lightly touches my arm. "Noelle? You still
with us?"

My instinct is to snap at her, but I push it down. Growth. Sort of.

"Yep, sorry." When I look back at the network folk, they're watching me warily. Shit. "Look, I'm sorry. This isn't how I usually act, especially to strangers. I'm just really protective of this town and worried about how this is going to impact my business. I promise I'm usually pretty nice—ask anyone. Well, maybe not anyone," I tack on, thinking about the woman beside me.

I shouldn't have bothered; Shay is a better person than I am and immediately jumps in to back me up.

"She really is. Everyone loves Noelle," Shay says, and it doesn't sound like she's forcing herself. Which, of course, makes me feel worse. "But you have to understand how important Wintermore is to everyone here. This town means so much to everyone who lives here, and we just want to make sure the town and the people are respected."

It's a perfect answer that has the network people relaxing, and me more tense than ever. Why is she, of all people, defending me? Being tired and stressed isn't an excuse to be an asshole, though it is the reason I'm acting like I have been to the people working on the movie. To Shay, though? That's how I always am.

She's either an incredible liar, or this is just another example of her managing everything better than me.

At this point, I have to pick my battles, and I've already agreed to the movie, so I may as well stop being so difficult about that. Besides, I do believe that this will be good for Wintermore as a whole. My family's businesses might be doing well, but I owe it to the town to do whatever I can to make sure everyone is thriving —even if I have to work myself to the bone to do it.

As for Shay being so nice… I can unpack that later.

I take a deep breath and make my shoulders relax. "I'd love to hear your plans for splitting your time between the two bakeries, and what kinds of things you'd like me and Shay to work on."

Relief shines from the faces of the network people, and I force a smile onto my own.

The redhead in the middle claps her hands. "Well, let's get started, shall we? The plan is simple…"

The plan is anything but simple.

I walk away from the meeting more exhausted than when I went in. Shay walks quietly beside me, and I have no idea what she makes of everything.

They're going to film in *Épices et Sucré* first, since Shay is happy to close completely and work on her orders from my basement kitchen, like we discussed. The Enchanted Bakery will operate as normal and close for one week right before the movie wraps so they can film whatever they need to film. I think the appeal of having a fully operational café and bakery in town for the crew, and the 25 percent discount I offered for anyone working on the movie, was the main driver there.

My team will continue to work in the main kitchen, and I'll work there until lunchtime, when I'll move to the basement to work on the ridiculous list of things the network wants for the movie.

The list they've given us ahead of time is only the items they know they want in advance. We've been warned that they'll likely double the amount while filming, and they'll need duplicates of most things. The baking itself should be relatively straightforward; I half expected them to ask us to decorate Styrofoam cakes and fake cookies to make filming easier, but they want the real thing for "authenticity." At least the crew will eat well.

Since the movie features two bakers, they want to see both my decorating style and Shay's reflected, which is a relief. I really don't want to have to learn a whole new style overnight if I don't have to.

Technically, as long as we stay on schedule—or get ahead—we should be able to take one day off a week, but I don't remember the last time I actually managed a full day off, so I doubt it.

We have a dedicated contact on the crew to help us coordinate everything, free rein to request whatever we need to make things work, and exactly six days until they start filming. Six days to prepare myself to spend over a month stuck in a kitchen with Shay.

I don't know what the hell I've gotten myself into.

"The plan is simple." Liars.

There's a tension headache sinking its claws behind my eyes, and I pinch the bridge of my nose.

"Are you okay?" Shay's voice is softer than usual, like she's deliberately lowering it because she realizes my head is sore.

"I'm fine." There's no heat left in me to put behind my words, which is just as well. "It's just… What the fuck were they talking about, calling the plan simple?" I groan.

Shay sucks in a breath. "I know, right? Simple plans don't usually require ten pages of instructions." She brandishes the bundle of papers they gave each of us after we signed the contracts. "Do you think we can make it work?"

I glance over at her. She's worrying her lip between her teeth, her gray eyes ever so slightly wide, like she's stressed about this all, too.

"Yeah," I answer, finally. "I think we can make it work. It's going to be exhausting, but we can do it."

My words seem to reassure her, tension I didn't notice leaving her shoulders with one deep breath. The setting sun swathes her in a golden glow, catching the brighter strands of her blonde hair and making them sparkle.

I look away, focusing on the crispy leaves on the sidewalk instead.

"I'll set up a calendar and add you so we can both access it on our phones and we can keep track of the bakes for the movie," I suggest, hugging my arms to my chest. "We can check in at the end of every day to see how we're getting on, and if we need to move anything around as they add more things to the list."

"That sounds perfect. Thank you," Shay answers, sounding grateful.

"What's your number?" I ask, pulling out my phone and starting a new contact.

Shay recites her number, then her email address, and I fill in her contact information. It only takes a few taps of my screen to set the calendar up and send the invite, and I spend every second wondering what kind of parallel universe I've stepped into where I now have a shared calendar with Shay Harland. Wild.

"Thanks," she says, accepting the calendar invite just as we reach her door. "I'll go through the list tonight and add everything they've given us to the calendar, then maybe we can find a day to go through it and decide who's working on what?"

"That would be helpful," I answer.

She leans against the brick wall, pocketing her phone. I don't know why I expect her to say goodbye and rush off. I've spent enough time around Shay recently to have learned that she never seems to be rushing, not like I am.

On a logical level, I know Shay's a nice person. I've never heard anyone say a bad word about her, other than that she keeps to herself. But I've never given her the chance to be nice to me, because I've refused to spend any time around her. The past week is shaking the, admittedly made-up, impression of her I've been clinging to.

"I know this is all last-minute and stressful, but I'm excited to get to work with you, Noelle," she says with a blinding smile. It feels a little like staring straight at the sun, and I struggle to hold her gaze.

I have no idea what to say to that, or what to make of the way it makes my stomach dip, so I just lift a hand, turn on my heel, and walk away.

8
SHAY

When Noelle said I'd be working in a basement kitchen, I expected something dark and dingy. I should've known better. This is bigger and better than the kitchen in my apartment.

There are a few small windows and a door as promised, but it's still a basement. I'm not entirely comfortable, but I've been worse. The sheer size of the room helps. There are two large islands, tons of storage, four ovens, and a giant fridge/freezer. Everything is brand-new, after Noelle had it renovated over the summer. And that's just the kitchen—there's a walk-in storage room I haven't braved. She mentioned something about the door getting stuck, and I'm not ready to risk that.

I asked her why she hasn't used the kitchen yet, and she looked like she wanted to bite my head off as she told me she's planning to hire more staff and use this kitchen over the holiday period, but hasn't had time. I forced down my instinct to offer help because, though Noelle has been less frosty with me lately, I can tell she's not happy about it. She moves between hot and cold at lightning speed.

I'd be lying if I said I wasn't enjoying trying to figure her out. There's something about Noelle that makes me want to peel away her layers and unwrap the mystery of her.

The polished granite is cool beneath my fingers as I run my hands over the countertop. It's all so perfect, it's hard to know where to start. I understand Noelle's concerns, but for me, taking on a new project, in a new space, with a new person, is exciting. Though right now, it's a little quiet.

I started working in my first kitchen when I was fifteen. It was a cramped little diner with no A/C and a half-dozen people too many, at any given time. I worked on pancakes, waffles, and pies every Sunday morning through the post-church rush, and I fell in love with the hustle and bustle of the kitchen.

Over the years, I've worked in more bakeries, restaurants, and patisseries than I can count, but *Épices et Sucré* is the first place I've ever worked alone. I'm used to absorbing the energy of those around me, and I love watching people work and learning from their skills. Working alone is… well, lonely. And quiet.

I set up my spare phone to film B-roll, take a deep breath that's too loud in the too quiet basement, and pull my tablet toward me. Sometimes, when I'm feeling particularly lonely in my kitchen, I put on the Food Network, or one of the bakers I like on YouTube, so it feels like I'm working alongside someone.

Today, I turn on one of Noelle's old lives. She's making dark chocolate cherry brownies with a salted pretzel base, but I'm more interested in watching her bake than I am in what she's baking. It's good to know who I'll be working with.

Everything she does seems to be almost instinctive. She weighs her ingredients, but all of her estimates are perfect. Her hands move smoothly over her workspace, cleaning up spills before they settle, returning to whatever she was working on a second before. It all just seems so natural.

It would be easy to assume it was an act for the camera, but something tells me otherwise. It's clear she loves her craft. The comments all mirror my thoughts, noting how easy she makes it look. She has a recipe in the video description, and a lot of the commenters have tried and loved it. Some even mention looking forward to visiting the bakery.

Noelle is a light that draws people in, like moths to a flame. And maybe that part is a lucky hand—luck for her parents choosing to move her, luck for being beautiful and personable—but even if they come for Noelle, they stay for her baking. I haven't disliked a single thing I've tried from The Enchanted Bakery, and while I know she's not making everything herself, she's pretty open online about all of her recipes being her own, and it's clear she holds her team to a high standard.

If I take the stress of the movie and my tentative excitement to be working with someone for a change out of the equation, mostly I'm just excited to get to see her bake in person.

I don't even realize I've been doing nothing but staring at my screen for an hour until she's saying goodbye, and my tablet auto-plays the next video. If I don't cut myself off, I'm going to get nothing done. Leaning over my notebook, I write out a plan of attack for the day. I'm a pen and paper person. I need to feel my plans flowing from a pen so they sink into my head, and I always sketch out my designs before I start working on them. On today's to-do list, I have three of my extra-large macaron cakes, a passion fruit pavlova, and a pear tarte tatin, and I need to start prepping some of the smaller things for my afternoon teas. Since *Épices et Sucré* is closed, I've opened up orders for at-home afternoon teas for this coming weekend, and they've been pretty popular.

The studio requested I leave everything I could in my kitchen, which wasn't too difficult considering Noelle has this place stocked, but I brought a few of the things I can't live without: my favorite spatulas, my emotional support mixing bowl, and my tiny step stool. Noelle has to be a good five or six inches taller than me, and I know she stores things up high.

Unlike the kitchen and café upstairs, the basement is surprisingly not Christmas themed. Maybe she just hasn't gotten around to sprinkling her festive magic down here.

I have about three hours before Noelle is due to come down here to work on our list for the movie, and a lot to squeeze in. I switch from the video to music and lose myself in sugar and flour.

9
NOELLE

"Is there a reason you're hanging out with me instead of doing the job I know you don't have time to be procrastinating?" my brother asks, crossing his arms and leaning back against a metal storage shelf filled with blind boxes. They've become some of The Enchanted Workshop's biggest sellers since Felix and Abigail started doing live packaging videos and opening the occasional blind box on camera. They have quite the following.

"I'm not procrastinating. I'm just… avoiding work."

Felix raises an eyebrow, not even bothering to respond.

We get along a lot better now that we don't work together, but he's right to be confused about my presence. I don't get time off during the day—I'm lucky if I get five minutes to grab lunch—and, if I did, I would probably spend it catching up on sleep or screaming into a pillow instead of hanging around my brother. And I wouldn't choose to spend it here.

I grew up in this store; it means everything to me and my family. But now, it serves as a reminder that, while I was running The Enchanted Workshop, I was managing. I was happy. I was dreaming. I was excited.

And now… Yeah.

"It's my first day working with Shay," I admit, toying with the string of the apron I forgot to take off before coming here. "I'm supposed to meet her in the basement kitchen"—I check my phone—"twenty minutes ago."

"It's not like you to be late," he points out, and I sigh, because he's right. I've always maintained that if you're not twenty minutes early, you're late.

"Right. But I don't want to do it, so…"

"Why'd you agree if you didn't want to do it so badly?"

"It didn't feel like I had a choice," I grumble. "I love this town, but do you ever feel an intense pressure to be your best self for everyone else here, since they've done so much for our family?"

Felix tilts his head, squinting, like he's mulling it over. "If I did, I wouldn't have spent so many years fucking around not doing my job. But you're not me, Noelle, and that's a good thing. The concept of responsibility is still pretty new to me."

God, what it must be like to be a man.

"You know, I'm sorry for putting so much extra pressure on you for so long when you were running this place," Felix adds, tapping the toe of his boot on the floor. Why the hell he's wearing cowboy boots is beyond me. We were born in Texas, but cowboy boots aren't really our family's vibe. "I'm guessing spending so long having the weight of everything on your shoulders alone has only added to the pressure. I'm trying to do better."

"I know you are. We can all see that. You *are* doing better."

"Right, but I guess what I'm saying is, this is your turn to enjoy yourself. And if you're not, you should find a way to," he finishes with a shrug.

It's not like Felix to take accountability, but I suppose that's part of trying to do better. Still, I didn't expect a heart-to-heart when I chose here to procrastinate. Felix and I have an understanding that we *don't* call each other on our shit. Rora? Blunt as all hell. She's who I go to when I need someone to tell me to get my shit together.

But Felix doesn't comment on me being miserable living my dream, and I don't comment on the way his gaze always lingers a second longer than it should on his best friend's little sister. It benefits neither of us in the long run, but both of us in the moment.

I clear my throat and look away from him. "True. Anyway, I should go." I'm not in the mood to open up to him—or anyone—so I suppose that's one way to get me to stop procrastinating.

If he says anything as I flee the toy store's storage room, I don't hear him. I wave goodbye to Abigail on my way out, taking a sharp right down the alley that runs between The Enchanted Workshop and The Enchanted Bakery. The basement door is open, and I can hear music blaring as I skip down the steps, preparing myself for an afternoon in the kitchen with Shay.

But nothing could have prepared me for any of this.

The first thing I notice is the mess. It's not dirty, but my god, it's cluttered. There are bowls, utensils, cooling racks, and decorations all over Shay's island and the countertops. I'm surprised she hasn't crept over to my island. The sink is empty, but there are dishes stacked beside it.

The second thing I notice is... her. She didn't strike me as a music fan, but Shay is dancing around, singing along to Fleetwood Mac as she sprinkles edible glitter over a giant macaron. Her hair is clipped back, but I can picture it swinging around like golden rays of sun. Something about her swaying her hips to "Dreams" is captivating. I can't look away—which is just as well, because if I have to look at the mess again, I might pass out.

I wait for her to put the glitter down to clear my throat, and thank god I did, because she jumps out of her skin, her hand flying to her chest.

"Fuck. You scared the shit out of me," she says, her cheeks turning pink.

"Sorry," I answer, taking a step into the kitchen.

Shay turns the music down, and I have no choice but to take in the mess before me.

"What's all this?" I ask, gesturing vaguely to the room.

"All of…" Shay trails off, looking at the island before her.

"Yeah, that. The general vibe of an asteroid hitting the kitchen?"

"Sorry," she says, a guilty expression crossing her face. "I tend to work in a pretty chaotic way and then clean up at the end of the day. I find the cleaning relaxing. I'm guessing you don't work like this?"

I set my bag gently by my island, leaning on the cool granite. "I don't know how anyone works like this. How do you find anything?"

"I have a system," she says quickly. Her elbow catches a bottle of what looks like almond extract, and it tumbles to the ground. Thankfully, the cap is on, but I'm starting to understand how she spilled an entire bottle of food coloring. "I'll do a better job of keeping the mess to my island," she says as she picks it up, and no part of me believes that's possible.

But, in the interest of being as nice as possible on our first day working together, I don't say that.

"Are you ready to get started on the movie stuff?" I ask instead, and she nods eagerly.

"Absolutely. Just give me two minutes to make some space."

Two minutes? Now this I *have* to see.

I watch, somewhat awed, as Shay stacks dishes and bakes with expert precision. I can tell she's done this before by the speed at which her hands move, sorting things into categories: food dye, sprinkles, ingredients, produce. I've got to hand it to her, because she has everything stacked neatly by the two-minute mark.

It's not *not* impressive, but more impressive would be not making a mess at all, in my opinion.

She rounds her island so she's standing on the other side of mine and drops a worn notebook on the countertop. For the first time, I notice the pencil tucked behind her ear.

It's kind of hot. And I hate that I'm thinking about it.

"So, how has your day been?" Shay asks, and I'm so distracted by the pencil that it takes me a second to process the question. And when I do, the only word my mouth manages to form is: "Huh?"

Shay gives me a warm smile. "Have you had a good day? Busy?"

"Um, yeah. It's been fine. Medium busy, I guess," I answer, trying not to show how much I really don't want to do this. If someone had told me two weeks ago that I'd be small-talking with Shay, I'd have assumed hell was about to freeze over. "How has your day been?" I ask because it's the polite thing to do.

I don't hear a word of Shay's answer, though, because she pulls the pencil out from behind her ear and twirls it in her fingers. In fact, I don't even notice she's stopped talking until she clears her throat.

"So… yeah. That was my day."

"Great," I say, hoping it *was* great, or I'm going to seem like even more of an asshole than usual. "Let's get started."

Shay flips open her notebook, and I grab my tablet from my bag on the floor. I've always been a digital planner—I love the ease of moving things around as I need to—and I'd be lying if I said I hadn't enjoyed trying to plan out my schedule between The Enchanted Bakery and the movie work. Seeing how little free time I have? Awful. But seeing everything come together on my screen? An unbeatable feeling.

I have everything color-coded, estimated times for every task, and a supply list that auto-updates when I paste the recipes I'm working on to it, split into my business expenses and the expenses I need to invoice the network for.

Shay has a checklist with a diagram of the cross-section of some kind of layered cake sketched out right in the middle of the page.

"It's a white chocolate and yuzu millefeuille," she says, noticing my gaze. "I've been testing the recipe for a few weeks, but it's missing something I haven't been able to put my finger on until today."

"What was it?"

"Wasabi. Just a little, but it ties it all together." Her eyes light up when she talks about baking, and I miss that feeling. I haven't had time to develop a new recipe in months, let alone play around with things like yuzu and wasabi. It's a lot of chocolate, peppermint, and gingerbread around here.

"Sounds nice. A lot more interesting than…" I peer at the list of bakes we have to get to the network by mid-week. "Sugar cookies, pumpkin cupcakes, and pecan pie."

Shay wrinkles her nose. "I hate pecan pie. Why would anyone choose pecan over apple or cherry?"

I also hate pecan pie, but I don't want to bond over our shared dislike.

"Why don't I get started on the sugar cookie dough, and you can get started on the pie dough? Then we can get them chilling while we work on the rest."

"Sounds good. Are you a music person while you bake? Or a podcast person? You strike me as a podcast person."

I swap my apron for a clean one from the back of the door, and frown over my shoulder. Shay is already pulling a clean mixing bowl toward her—where did she find so many bowls?—and weighing flour.

"I'm not a podcast person."

She looks up at me, frowning. "What do you listen to while you work?"

My own racing thoughts reminding me of all the things I have to do doesn't feel like the right answer, so I just shrug. "Music's fine."

Shay hits play on her playlist and sings along to every. Single. Song.

Tomorrow, I'm bringing headphones.

10
NOELLE

When I was planning the basement kitchen, storage was my number one priority. I specifically told my contractor that I wanted more storage space than I could possibly need, and I was sure we'd achieved that. For the past few months, this kitchen has been a game changer—we keep bulk ingredients, equipment, and packaging down here, and only what we need on hand for the day upstairs.

But I never accounted for trying to squeeze an entire movie production's worth of *extra* supplies in here.

For the last couple of days, Shay and I have been using our own ingredients. With everything being so last minute, it took the crewperson tasked with ordering everything a few days to get it all in. Thankfully, between the two of us, we had enough on hand to get started on some more basic stuff.

It's been nice to actually get to bake again—I spend so much time doing everything else for The Enchanted Bakery, and I've found myself looking forward to getting stuck back into a mixing bowl the past couple of days. Today, however, has been the day from hell.

I was supposed to finish up with The Enchanted Bakery at lunchtime, but I ended up spending the whole day working on social media, cleaning the café floor thanks to the raging storm outside, doing admin, and putting out fires (literally). I didn't even get the chance to tell Shay in person—I texted her that I'd be late and not to wait around for me. But when I finally make it downstairs to the basement kitchen, I find her standing in a maze of boxes.

"Holy shit."

Shay jumps, like she was staring so intently at the boxes that she didn't hear me come in. "I know, right? I went home to eat dinner, and when I came back…" She shakes her head, looking wide-eyed at the piles and piles of stuff. She holds up a stapled bundle of paper. "They left an inventory and a note asking us to check everything."

So much for baking.

I close the door behind me, blocking out the howling wind. I almost want to ignore it and suggest we deal with it later, but Shay looks a little flushed, and I remember what she said about being claustrophobic. Being in the basement with the door closed while it's stormy must be hard enough, let alone being stuck with no room to move.

"Let's get this done quickly." I hold out my hand. "I'll take the list, you check the boxes," I suggest, because that seems like it'll distract her more.

Shay passes me the papers, and we slowly but surely check things off the list. She has a knack for finding things in the sea of boxes that *almost* impresses me.

"Thirty pounds of semi-sweet chocolate chips—four boxes."

"Got 'em."

"Two boxes of white chocolate?"

"They're here."

"Ten pounds of shredded coconut, and ten pounds of flakes."

"Yep."

"Two dozen cans of pear halves in juice."

Shay is quiet for so long that I look up from the list. She

squints at the boxes, crouching down and rummaging through them.

"I don't see any cans. Maybe they saw the other cans in the pantry and put them there?"

"I'll check."

I hop over a big package of paper towels and dodge boxes on my way to the pantry. Sure enough, there are more supplies. A *lot* more supplies. I squeeze into the pantry, surrounded on all sides by more stuff.

The curse that spills from my mouth is unintentional, but not unwarranted.

I hear a scuffle, and a moment later, Shay appears in the doorway. "Are you oh—holy shit."

She stares at the stacks of cans and cartons, open-mouthed.

"Where the hell are we going to put all this?" she asks, and I shrug, because I certainly don't have the answers. She must see on my face how close I am to spiraling, because she quickly kneels down and continues, "We can probably stack these all more efficiently to save space. I'll read out what we have, and you can check them off."

"Sure."

She calls out the can contents and quantities by the door, and I do my job, checking them off while she re-stacks them into slightly more organized piles. She slides them closer together, saving all of an inch of space, but it's something.

Shay brushes the knees of her jeans. "We should take a coffee break. It's going to be a long night."

I agree, dropping the list and pen on top of the nearest box. I pull my phone out of my pocket to check the time, not paying attention to Shay as she stands up.

Until I hear a loud clank and an "ouch" as Shay's toe connects with the wooden wedge holding the door open.

I look up, eyes wide. "Be careful. Don't let it—"

I'm too late. Shay's boot must have dislodged the stopper, and the door is too heavy, too fast, for her to grab it in time.

It closes with a loud thunk, plunging us into darkness. My phone and the crack between the door and the uneven stone floor are the only lights.

Shay immediately rushes forward, desperately trying to find the handle and tugging the door, but I already know it won't budge.

Shit.

"Noelle." Her voice is shaky, cracking on the second syllable. "Can you help me, please? I need… Fuck, I need to get out of here. I can't… Please."

My heart races, more at Shay's panic than the enclosed space. I move slowly toward her, trying not to panic her further.

She jumps out of her skin when I place a hand on her shoulder, turning her gently toward me.

"I need you to breathe, Shay. Copy me, okay?"

I take a deep breath, but she's shaking, and I'm not sure she even hears it.

"I can't… I can't breathe. Please, Noelle. Help me open the door."

I swallow, dreading her reaction to what I have to say. Steeling myself, I squeeze her shoulder. "I'm here, and I've got you. But it doesn't open. We—"

"What?" The word is a high-pitched sob, and Shay's body lurches, like she's going to pass out.

I don't think; I just wrap my arms around her, holding her steady.

"The door is broken. It can only be opened from the outside," I explain, trying to keep my voice even. If I sound as worried as I feel, that's only going to make her panic more.

"We're stuck in here? Oh god."

She's crying, and every gasp digs a deeper pit in my stomach.

"I'm going to call someone to come get us out. It's going to be okay."

I take her hand and place it directly over my chest so she can feel the rise and fall. It's clammy, her fingers trembling. It feels like she's barely holding herself up.

"Try and match your breathing to mine."

"Okay," she replies, half-hiccup, half-sob.

I pull out my phone. Since the café and the basement doors are both closed, I'm limited to the people who have keys for The Enchanted Bakery. My parents, Felix, Rora, and Henry. There's never been a need for any of the staff to have keys, because I live right upstairs.

My parents are staying at Rora's cabin for a few days, and cell reception is spotty up there. Felix is closest, so I call him first. His cell rings out three times. I grit my teeth as I listen to the start of his voicemail message again—god forbid he answer his phone when I actually need him. The toy store closed an hour ago, but I try it anyway, to no avail.

Rora and Henry are our last shot.

I try not to let my worry show as I dial. Shay's breathing is getting more erratic with every call that goes unanswered. I place my hand over hers on my chest, stroking my thumb slowly over the back of her hand.

"Hey. What's up?"

I could cry as my best friend's voice sounds down the line. "Hi." My voice sounds foreign to my own ears—too forced, too cheery, too loud in the hushed pantry. And Rora notices right away.

"What's wrong?"

"Shay and I are stuck in the pantry in the basement. Can you come let us out, please?"

Rora whistles. "Shit. I mean, yeah, but we're in Jackson, so we'll be an hour and a half at least." *Fuck.*

Shay must be able to hear, because she lets out a sob that has me tightening my hold on her.

"Was that Shay? Is she okay?" Rora asks, sounding alarmed.

"Everything's fine!" I'm not even convincing myself at this point. "Shay's a little claustrophobic, but she's doing okay. Aren't you?" I prompt, squeezing her hand.

"I'm okay," she says, sounding anything but.

I hear Rora ushering my uncle Henry to start the car. "Did you try Felix?"

"He's not picking up," I reply through gritted teeth. "Can you guys drive quickly?"

"We'll be there as soon as we can," Rora promises.

I focus on Shay when I hang up, rummaging around in my pocket. I don't have tissues, but I have a napkin from the samples I was checking this morning. It'll do.

I'm not sure what possesses me to wipe her cheeks myself, instead of handing it to her, but she presses her face against my hand, like the touch is comforting.

"They'll be here soon," I tell her, wiping gently. "You're doing great."

"Thank you," she hiccups. "I'm sorry about this. It hasn't… It hasn't been this bad in a while."

"You don't need to apologize. Is there anything I can do to make it better?"

She shakes her head. "I just need to get out of here. I've tried so many things over the years—hypnotherapy, medication, meditation, and nothing helps." Every word is punctuated with a gulp of air.

"Have you always been claustrophobic?"

"Since the accident," Shay replies, her voice barely louder than a whisper. The accident. Her sister.

I open my mouth to tell her she doesn't need to talk about it, but she continues, "Nico was driving. Georgie was in the front—

she always called shotgun, even when we were too old to be doing it. We were going to meet our parents for dinner, and it was stormy, like it is today, but worse. It was windy, and we'd had a lot of bad storms, so the roads were a mess. Nico's a great driver, but it happened so quickly, there was nothing he could do. A rockfall. It would've been okay if the barrier at the edge of the road hadn't been damaged in the storms, but we went over the side and fell down a ravine. Eleven hours, we were trapped there."

Horror curdles my stomach, but Shay seems to calm down as she talks about it. Her breathing slowly evens out, her fingers still a statue against my chest.

"The car hit front first," she continues. "I got so lucky; I wasn't even knocked unconscious. But Nico and Georgie were. I can't explain it, but I knew. I knew Nico was alive, and I knew Georgie wasn't. They said she probably died instantly, but they had no way of knowing for sure. I did, though. I knew. I felt it. Nico didn't wake up, and I couldn't move to get help, so I just screamed until I lost my voice. He wasn't conscious, but he swears he heard me—that he remembers me screaming, begging, praying. I didn't even remember, but he did."

"How did they find you?" I ask. I think Shay is shaking again, until I realize it's me.

"A runner spotted the car the next morning. Nico was in a coma for a few days, and I wasn't as lucky as I thought. I had a tear in my spleen and was slowly bleeding out. If they'd found us even two hours later, I probably would've died. But I didn't."

The words "Georgie did" are unspoken, but so loud.

"I'm so sorry, Shay."

She sniffs, and I can't put into words how much the soft laugh that spills from her calms my pounding heart.

"No, no. I'm sorry. I didn't mean to trauma dump on you. Just distracting myself, I guess."

Her spine tenses, like she suddenly remembers where we are.

"I can distract you," I say, quickly following it up with, "That sounded a lot more suggestive than I meant it to."

She huffs a long breath, but at least she's breathing better. "Will you tell me about your family? How you all ended up obsessed with Christmas?"

"Yeah. I can do that," I say, holding her tight. She doesn't seem to mind, and I'm not sure I can let go of her.

11

SHAY

The storm has settled a little by the time Rora and Henry unlock the pantry door. I've settled too. I'm not surprised Noelle is so good at calming people down, but I am surprised she was willing to do it for me.

She insists on walking me home, ignoring my protests when I try to stay to put everything away. We didn't get very far. Rora and Henry offer to stay and help—Sunny is asleep in her car seat, ironically soothed by the storm that's the opposite of her namesake.

Noelle holds my arm as we cross the street. There's no one around; everyone is probably hiding out after the storm. I hope this doesn't set filming back.

Something has shifted between me and Noelle tonight. We're not friends by any stretch of the imagination, but maybe working together will be a little less... fraught. I don't know what came over me. I never open up to anyone about the accident. The last person I told was Philippe, and he admitted that talking about it made him uncomfortable, so I just stopped bringing it up. Noelle just listened. It was oddly refreshing.

She walks me up the stairs, watching until I open my front door. Cat is nowhere to be seen. I hope he's curled up inside, and not out in the storm.

"Do you have food?" Noelle asks, hovering by the door.

"Yeah. I already ate, though."

"Right. Well, rest up. And if you need anything…" She trails off, short of offering. Understandably so—we're in uncharted waters here. Noelle clears her throat. "I'll see you tomorrow."

"See you tomorrow."

She starts down the stairs but pauses when I call her name. "Yeah?"

"Thank you for today."

Her expression softens for a split second, then it's gone. She nods, turning and running across the street. I watch her go, a blur of lilac in the blue night.

I find Cat curled up like a croissant on my bed. I quickly get ready for bed, leaving a trail of mess behind me—I'm too tired to tidy—and lie beside him, pulling him closer, and kissing the top of his head. He meows, either in greeting or in indignation at me waking him up, and rubs his face against mine.

He falls asleep in my arms while I toss and turn. Every time I close my eyes, I hear the howl of the wind. The impact of the rocks. The crunch of the car. Georgie's scream, suddenly silenced. I smell the smoke. The blood. The salt from the tears that poured down my cheeks until they ran out.

But I also remember the feel of Noelle's fingers on my cheek as she wiped my tears. The steady rise and fall of her chest beneath my hand. The brown sugar, gingerbread scent she emanates. The soft cadence of her voice, the soothing sound of her breathing.

"I'm here, and I've got you."

I'm too exhausted to unpack the way those words echo in my mind—the way they're the last thing I think about before I finally drift off.

12

NOELLE

I've never seen someone carve the peel from a lemon so intensely. Honestly, I've just never seen anyone work so intensely in a kitchen, period.

There are a hundred things I should be doing, but I'm falling behind on my to-do list because I can't stop watching Shay. At first, I just wanted to make sure she was okay after last night. Intense doesn't even begin to cover it. It can't have been easy to open up about the accident like she did, to talk about her sister, but she seems fine today. Maybe a little more tired than she usually is—I spotted several takeout cups from The Frosty Bean in the recycling when I came in. Otherwise, she seems right as rain.

Once I confirmed that, it should've been easy to look away, but I can't.

It's not like she's doing or making anything particularly exciting; she's just doing it in a way that could only be described as… captivating. She narrows her eyes, focusing solely on whatever she's working on, her lips pursed. I've never noticed how small her hands are, how delicate her fingers are. Why would I have? But now that I have noticed them… God, I think I'm losing it.

I turn my attention back to the bowl of cookie dough before me. Triple chocolate, with crushed pretzels and big flakes of coconut. It smells divine. No matter how long I've been baking, I never tire of stealing a bite of cookie dough as I'm scooping it. I know people say you shouldn't, but life is too short to worry about raw cookie dough.

In the three and a half days we've worked together, I've tried to get a grasp on Shay's music taste, but I can't. It's all over the shop, from country, to '90s boy bands, to R&B, to musical theater, to ABBA. There's a lot of ABBA, actually. I would confidently guess that they're her favorite band, and based on the number of times "Lay All Your Love On Me" shows up on her playlists, and the way she can't stop herself from swaying when it does, I would guess this is her favorite song.

I let my gaze dance over her body as I scoop the cookies and sprinkle them with sea salt. She moves slowly, softly mouthing the words. I zero in on her lips, on the sweet pink blush. She always wears a sheer brown lip balm that smells like coffee—I know because it's so strong I can smell it when she's putting it on—and looking at her lips as she sings along to ABBA, I can't help but wonder if it tastes as good as it smells. If Shay tastes as good as she smells.

The thought stops me in my tracks, like I've been doused in scalding water. I still, my hand hovering over the cookies, my eyes glued to her lips.

I do *not*, under any circumstances, want to taste Shay fucking Harland. Not now, not ever.

This is just the past week, month, year, catching up with me. I'm tired—I didn't get to bed until two this morning, after putting everything away. I need to lay off the caffeine and the cookie dough and sleep more. Maybe I need to go for a walk by the reservoir and literally touch grass. Maybe I need a girls' night with Rora, where we look up all the people we went to high school with online to see what they're doing now. What I don't need is to kiss Shay.

I shouldn't even be *thinking* about kissing Shay.

Because she's Shay. Fucking. Harland.

"Noelle?"

I jolt back into awareness, realizing I've been staring so intently at Shay's lips that I missed whatever she said. "Huh?"

"I asked if the music is too loud? I can turn it off."

"Yes," I snap. It comes out harsher than I intended, and a small crease appears between Shay's brows. This is good. I need to remind both of us that I don't like her. Last night was… I don't fucking know what last night was. All I know is that less music means less of Shay dancing, and maybe I'll be able to concentrate better.

Shay recovers quickly, a pretty smile spreading across her mouth. "Sure!" She turns the music off and sets her paring knife aside in favor of something bigger to slice the peel into tiny ribbons.

I finish sprinkling the salt and cover the trays with plastic wrap before sliding them into the freezer. We'll bake them the day they need them on set. In hindsight, I should probably have waited to salt them until baking, but I—

"What are you doing?" I cross my arms, glaring at Shay as she closes her lips around a spoon.

"Tasting the batter," she says, her tongue darting out to catch a drop the spoon left behind on her lip. "You want to try it? It's really good."

"You shouldn't eat raw flour or eggs." I'm a goddamn hypocrite.

"One bite won't hurt," Shay replies with a soft, twinkly laugh and… a wink. I bite the inside of my cheek and turn away, the sharp burst of pain doing nothing to ground me.

Who just winks like that?

I was so worried I wouldn't be able to hide how much I dislike Shay while we're working together, but apparently, I was worried about the wrong damn thing. This is bad.

This is *so* fucking bad.

I grab my phone from my apron pocket and sigh when I notice the time. I was hoping to get in a couple more hours, to get ahead, so I might be able to take a little longer off on Sunday for family dinner, but I have to get out of here.

Shay hums along to her music while I clean up, making quick work of putting everything away and wiping down the counters. Thank god I'm a tidy-as-I-go kind of baker, because there's not a lot for me to do. It's tempting to half-ass my end-of-day routine, but I know I'll regret it tomorrow if I do.

I check the dates of the fresh produce in the refrigerator, pulling forward anything that needs to be used tomorrow, refill my shakers with flour, powdered sugar, and cornstarch for dusting, sweep the floor under my workstation, and, most importantly, I don't look at Shay once.

All in, it takes me less than ten minutes to close out my workstation. And then I make a fatal mistake: I look up.

Shay has her back to me as she bends over the counter on the back wall, piping coffee ganache and salted caramel on the macaron shells she baked earlier. She's wearing blue jeans that hug her body like a dream, a white T-shirt, and a navy apron. The strings are looped around her back, framing a tiny sliver of skin that's visible where her T-shirt is riding up.

She finishes up her piping and drops the bag, tip and all, onto the big pile of mess that's been accumulating all afternoon by the sink. To give her her due, the kitchen is always spotless before she leaves, and she never complains about cleaning up. Honestly, she seems to like it. Shay does everything with a smile on her face and a pep in her step. The kind I used to have when I baked for fun, before this place sucked all the joy out of my one true love.

At least Shay is showing this kitchen a little joy these days. It sure as hell ain't getting it from me.

I don't recognize the song she's humming as she peers up at

the shelves above the counters, but every sound disappears from my head when she stands on her tiptoes and reaches up. Her T-shirt rides up, exposing a two-inch strip of her back, and I swear the breath is knocked from my lungs when I spy the edge of a tattoo. I can't tell what it is, but I see a flash of green and blue as she teeters on her toes.

The sight of her almost falling is enough to snap me back to my senses. Whatever she's trying to get, she's not tall enough to reach. Shay isn't short, but she's not as tall as I am, and this kitchen was built with my height in mind.

I cross the room, and every step toward her feels… dangerous. It's like every inch of floor I clear is going to make it that much harder to retreat.

And then I'm standing right behind her, and I can smell the lemon and the sugar and the white chocolate from the cake she made, and the coffee and caramel from the macarons, and the fresh daisy scent that always seems to hover around Shay. The combination overwhelms my senses, but I don't hate it.

"What are you trying to reach?" I ask, my voice low and hoarse.

Shay jumps, twisting her body until she's facing me, her eyes wide. "Shit. I didn't hear you coming over."

"Sorry," I offer, not sounding sorry at all, because this close, I can see the flecks of silver in her gray eyes. I can see the freckle on her lower lip. And as soon as I spot it, it's *all* I can see.

The polite thing to do would be to take a few steps back. The sensible thing to do would be to run the hell out of here. I do neither.

"Um…" Shay runs her tongue over her bottom lip, and I have to stop my knees from buckling. "The purple silicone mat."

"What?" I ask, barely hearing her.

"From the shelf. That's what I was trying to reach."

Right. That's why I came over here.

I reach for the mat, my fingers closing around the soft silicone with ease. I set it on the counter beside Shay, but she doesn't look at it. Her eyes are on mine, like she's searching the very depths of me.

"Thank you. Are you finished for the day?"

I nod, but everything feels like it's slowed down just a little. Like we're operating at 0.75 times speed. "Yeah. I'm all cleaned up, so I'm—"

"You missed a spot."

My eyes narrow in confusion. "What?"

Shay's pupils are impossibly black as she lifts her hand. "On your cheek. Cocoa powder, I think."

I hold my breath as she brushes my cheek with her thumb. I almost close my eyes, but she's looking up at me through thick lashes, and I can't physically look anywhere but into her eyes.

"Got it," she says, starting to pull her hand away.

I have no idea what possesses me, but I place my hand on top of hers, trapping it against my face. It's the opposite of the position we were in yesterday—physically, and in energy. Shay sucks in a breath as a myriad of emotions cross her face.

Confusion, surprise, intrigue, desire.

The last one is what my brain focuses on.

I feel out of my body, like I'm watching from a distance. I must be, because if I were truly present, there's no way in the world I would lean in closer to her.

Shay pulls her lip between her teeth, and a soft "fuck" tumbles from me before I can stop it.

"Noelle," she whispers, and it sounds like both a question and an answer.

My name on her lips shreds the final scrap of self-control I've been clinging to.

It happens in slow motion, and at lightning speed, all at once.

My fingers slide back from hers into her hair, and I close the distance between us, pressing my mouth to hers.

It's barely a touch; my lips brush hers for a split second at most, but Shay groans, and the sound strikes a match somewhere deep inside me.

What the fuck am I doing?

I jump back, putting three feet between us and leaving Shay staring at me, open-mouthed, her hair mussed and her cheeks rosy.

"Noelle—"

"I have to go." I don't give her a chance to respond. I turn on my heel and run out of the kitchen faster than I think I've ever run from anything before.

I kissed Shay fucking Harland.

I am *so* fucked.

13
SHAY

What the hell just happened?

I stare at the open door long after Noelle runs out of the basement, my heart thumping. My body has forgotten how to move, like the feeling of her lips against mine has wiped every other memory clean to set up a permanent spot in my brain.

A gust of wind blows the door until it bangs against the wall, jolting me out of my stupor. I make quick work of packing up my stuff, stopping the B-roll recording on my phone, and locking up the kitchen.

Should I go after her? Reassure her?

I don't even know what I'd say. And bolting like a bat out of hell is a pretty clear sign that Noelle doesn't want to talk to me right now.

So I drag my feet across the street and up the stairs to my apartment. Cat is waiting for me, immediately winding between my legs and trying to trip me up. He almost manages, too, since I'm so utterly shaken by the past twenty minutes.

I feed him and drop straight onto the couch, rubbing my face with my hands.

Noelle is the first person I've kissed since my ex-husband. She's the first woman I've kissed since before Georgie died. And it was…

Fuck.

I know I'm not straight, obviously. It's not like I haven't thought about it since Philippe and I got married, but every time I did, I pushed it down. What was the point in thinking about it when I was married to a man? If anything, I felt guilty when I did.

But I'm not married anymore. Of course, that doesn't make it okay for me to be thinking about a woman sixteen years younger than me, but… I'm thinking about it.

I've never been kissed like that in my life. It lasted all of five seconds, but her lips were soft but desperate, and her fingers fisted my hair like they'd been doing it forever. It was a perfect kiss—or it would've been, if she hadn't been so horrified with herself, and if it wasn't ridiculously fucking inappropriate.

My phone feels like a lead weight in my hand as I unlock it and open my camera roll. I click on the last video and scroll through the B-roll footage, steeling myself before hitting play.

A groan falls from my lips as I watch the kiss.

On camera, it's quick. One second, she's hovering in front of me; the next, her hands are clenched in my hair. Then she's gone, and I'm left standing there, stunned.

I slow the footage and watch it back so many times that I think it would be burned on the back of my eyelids if I could bear to close my eyes. With every watch, I remember the feel of her, the all-consuming ginger scent of her. I pick up on the little details: the way her hand flexes a second before she snaps, the way her eyes widen for a brief moment before she turns and runs… the way she stumbles at the door for all of a split second, like she's considering doubling back.

That tiny moment of hesitation is what sticks in my head the most.

That's the moment that has me finally swiping out of the video and opening Locked, where Noelle's profile is still waiting on my screen.

That's the moment that, good idea or bad, has me swiping on the big green button and sucking in a deep breath when the words "You're a Match!" flash up on my screen.

14
NOELLE

I'm not in the habit of kissing people I hate.

Hell, I'm not in the habit of hating people—or kissing people much these days.

I have no idea what came over me, other than, in that moment, I couldn't *not* kiss her. And what a kiss.

It was nothing, really. Our lips barely touched. But I can still feel the ghost of her, burned against my mouth.

Has she burrowed under my skin so easily because I've avoided spending time with her for so long? Was it the lingering effect of being trapped together? Or is this just Shay?

She's fucking with my head, and she's not doing anything beyond existing in my orbit. It's exhausting. I'm exhausted.

But one little kiss, and I'm… invigorated. Fuck. This is the last thing I need.

I've reached the point of no return where, like it or not, I have to admit it to myself: Shay Harland is fucking hot. She's also pretty nice. Nicer than I've treated her anyway, but I already knew that. She's never been the problem in that regard—my personal hang-ups are just that: personal.

So I have a crush. So what? I'm a thirty-year-old woman, I've had plenty of crushes in my lifetime, and, clearly, not a single one of them turned into anything worth a damn.

I wasn't a late-blooming lesbian by any means. When the girls in our class started talking about having crushes on boys, Rora and I would sit in my bedroom and wonder if there was something wrong with us. Until we watched *Grey's Anatomy,* and I dreamed about Addison Montgomery for a month straight. Rora dutifully watched it on repeat with me before admitting that she had a thing for Mark *and* Lexi. Formative experiences all around.

Growing up queer in Wintermore was better than most small towns. I'm sure comments were made, but my family is well respected, and if anyone did say anything, it never made it back to me. I had one girlfriend in high school—Mayor Blackwood's daughter—but the world opened up for me in college. I dated casually, and not so casually, and had my heart broken so many times. And every time, I thought it would never come back together.

I've had crushes on all kinds of women over the years, though never someone so much older than me, or someone that I claimed to hate. Maybe hate is too strong a word. In fact, it's possible I don't hate Shay as much as I thought I did. Or at all. I'm so goddamn confused.

Right now, the only person I hate is myself, because I had no business kissing Shay, and I had no business liking it so much.

The permanent exhaustion I'm so used to is mixed with a buzzing energy at the center point of my chest that makes me want to throw up as I finally make it into my apartment and lock the door behind me. I like peace, but not like this. It's too quiet, and I need something to shut out the screaming chorus of "What the fuck?" that's blaring in my head on repeat.

I find a package of spicy ramen at the back of my pantry and toss it in a pan with some water until it's cooked. I add a heaping spoonful of chili oil and crush up some uncooked noodles—I like the crunch—before devouring it. It does nothing to fill the empty space behind my ribs.

So I plant myself on the couch and pick up the sci-fi book

Felix has been nagging me to read for months, but I can't focus. I scrub my kitchen, sort my laundry, and water my plants until I run out of chores. I scroll through my phone until my feed blurs before my eyes, and I realize I'm not taking anything in.

Since I'm apparently all for admitting things to myself tonight, here's another: I've forgotten how to not work. I've forgotten how to leave the bakery at a reasonable hour and just relax. Unless I have a specific task pre-planned, I have no idea how to fill my time.

I waste twenty minutes on an everything shower with scalding water to distract me from my own thoughts, and another half hour giving myself a waste of a blowout, considering I'm going to have to put my hair up for work tomorrow. And it's still only eight p.m.

My bed is rarely made these days, and tonight is no exception. I have so little time to get ready before rushing to the bakery every morning, why bother? I climb under the rumpled covers and flick on my TV for the first time in I don't even know how long.

I snort when a rerun of *Grey's* is playing. Of fucking course.

The episode is from an early season, and I take none of it in as I stare at the screen. All I can think about is… her. Shay. How her lips felt, how her hair felt, how much I regret pulling away. If that's the only kiss we get—and it better be—then I really could've done more with it. I have to live the rest of my life knowing how soft her lips are, but not what she tastes like. Even the *Grey's Anatomy* writers couldn't come up with something so tragic.

She definitely kissed back. It was brief, it was nothing really, but she kissed me back. Was it just because she's so nice, or…

Or did she want me to kiss her? Is she sitting toiling over what the kiss could've been? Is she imagining what it would feel like to have my lips all over her, my tongue all over her?

I know so little about her, and now that I'm no longer denying this stupid little crush I have, what's the harm in looking her up?

I start with Facebook, expecting her profile to be locked down. But it's not. She doesn't post often—it's mostly someone, her mom, I think, sharing things to her feed and her commenting or liking.

I check out her *About* section, doing the math on her graduation year: she's either forty-six or forty-seven. She grew up in Oakland, California, practically right next door to Berkeley, where I went to college. Her parents still live there, from what I can tell. She has a few pictures from recent years, from trips home and a few family weddings. I find the pictures from *her* wedding. She had to have been younger than me when she got married. Philippe is her ex's name. She looks… resigned, in the pictures. Neither happy nor sad, just there. I've only met her brother in passing—I don't go up the mountain often, and he doesn't come down—but he hasn't changed much from what I can tell. He looks miserable in Shay's wedding pictures, like there's a dark cloud hanging over him. Which is exactly how he looks now, in my experience.

She was beautiful on her wedding day, she's beautiful in every picture on her feed, but they have nothing on the real thing. They don't capture the glow of her aura, the delicate intensity of every move she makes.

I throw my phone down, lying back with a groan, squeezing my eyes closed. Not even the picture in my head does her justice, but I can't get her out. Every inch of me is humming with electricity—wishing, wishing, wishing…

Fuck it.

I'd rather deal with the post-orgasm regret of getting off to the thought of Shay than this goddamn emptiness.

I kick off my underwear and spread my legs, running one hand up the inside of my old college T-shirt, and letting the other skate south. I take a deep breath, letting the image of her consume me, imagining how she feels, how she tastes.

Lemons, I decide. Lemons, and sugar, and vanilla, and sunshine. Sweet and tart, soft and rich.

My moan is too loud in the silence of the room as I brush my clit with one finger, but I can't hold it back. I try to imagine how she would touch me: slow, tentative, scrutinizing every reaction. She would do whatever it took to make it good for me, I know it.

And I know my fingers don't feel half as good as hers would.

I open my nightstand drawer and blindly pull out a toy, hoping it's charged and powerful. I'm not picky when it comes to sex toys. I like to try new things, so anything could be in there, but my hand closes around a basic suction toy.

Yes. Absolutely yes.

I breathe a sigh of relief when it buzzes to life, and an even bigger, happier sigh when I press it to my clit. There's no point in fucking around—it's been a long day, and I'm not interested in dragging this out. I turn up the speed, one, two, three, until I'm writhing in the sheets. My body twists, my head pressing back into the pillows as sparkles dance before my eyes, and all I can smell is lemon. It's easy to imagine the weight of Shay on top of me when I'm so out of my mind with lust, easy to imagine it's her lips around my clit and not an expensive piece of pink silicon.

So easy to imagine that I can practically feel her hair tickling my thighs. I can't open my eyes, but if I did, I bet I could imagine her between my legs, silver eyes looking up at me through her long lashes.

The vision in my head hits me like a freight train, and I come to the thought of Shay's mouth on me, with her name on my tongue. I press the toy harder against my clit, catching every aftershock as it rolls over my body like flames, biting my lip so hard I'm surprised I can't taste blood. My hips buck off the bed, my body rising with the orgasm and then falling, slowly, softly, like I'm floating on a cloud.

My phone chimes while I'm still trying to breathe through the dregs of the orgasm, and I reach clumsily for it, knocking it to the floor. Embarrassing.

I grumble as I have to lean down to grab it, and almost drop my phone again when I read the notification:

You have a match! Chat with Shay now!

What the fuck?

15
SHAY

I'm not saying that I stayed up later than is reasonable, watching my phone in case Noelle messaged me. But I'm not *not* saying that.

She did not message me. Clearly. Nor has she breathed a word about the kiss *or* the match since she came down to the basement kitchen to work a few hours ago, and the workday is almost over.

Six hours standing less than ten feet apart, and she's barely said a word to me. Not that that's unusual for Noelle, but after yesterday… I'm probably overthinking it. She regretted the kiss, that much was obvious. And maybe she has her notifications turned off for Locked and didn't see the match. Or maybe she did, and she's taking pity on me by not bringing up how not interested in me she is.

She sure felt interested yesterday. Before she ran like the wind, I guess.

Noelle is crumb coating a couple of cakes, and I sneakily watch her from behind my bowl of Italian meringue buttercream. I'm an almost forty-seven-year-old woman, acting like a high school freshman with a crush on the goddamn cheerleader. It's embarrassing.

I wonder if she was a cheerleader in high school. She doesn't seem like the type, but everything I know about Noelle is second-hand information passed on by a town that clearly sees her as a Whitten before they see her as Noelle.

"What were you like in high school?" I ask before I can stop myself.

Noelle's hand stills, the spatula she's holding dead center on top of the cake. "What? Why?" she asks without looking up.

"I'm just curious. You know, were you a band person, an athlete, a *math*lete?"

She sighs, spinning the cake on the turntable and smoothing out the crumb coat. "I was head elf of the Christmas Club."

At first, I think I've misheard her. Then, I think she must be fucking with me. But this *is* Wintermore…

"Please tell me you're joking."

"I'm not. Felix was head elf, and then he passed the baton to me. I also played the clarinet," she adds, as if to prove that Christmas wasn't her entire identity, "and I was salutatorian."

That part doesn't surprise me. No matter how little I know about her, I can tell she's smart—not to mention dedicated.

"Did you go to college?"

She grits her teeth, but she's entertaining my questions more than I expected her to, at least.

"I went to Berkley."

"You're kidding! I'm from Oakland," I say, cringing a little at how enthusiastic I sound, knowing we have something so small in common.

I don't expect Noelle to sound enthusiastic—I don't expect her to acknowledge it at all.

I *definitely* don't expect her to say, "I know. I looked you up on Facebook."

"I—Wha—When?" I pick my jaw up off the floor just in time for her to look up. Her expression is a mystery to me. Somehow, when it comes to Noelle, I always feel like I'm a step behind.

"Last night. After I kissed you, before you matched with me on Locked."

Well, there it is. I guess we're not ignoring the elephant in the room.

She doesn't ask if it was an intentional match. She probably doesn't have to, given how into the kiss I was.

"Are we going to talk about it?" I ask.

Noelle takes her time finishing the crumb coat and carrying the cake to the fridge to chill before answering. "The kiss? Or the matching?"

How can she sound so calm about all this? So unbothered. She starts cleaning up, and I follow suit, because I don't know how I'm supposed to get anything done when all I can think about is how her lips felt on mine yesterday in this exact spot.

"Both," I answer, as I scoop the meringue buttercream into a container and set my bowl beside the sink.

"I'm sorry. About the kissing, I mean. It's pretty out of character for me to kiss people I work with. Or people I don't... you know."

I round the island, leaning back against the cool worktop, and crossing my arms. "Why?"

"Why don't I kiss people?"

"Why don't you like me?" I ask bluntly, and Noelle looks at me, her eyes wide, like she didn't expect me to call her on it. Which, given my personality, is understandable. "Look," I continue, "I don't need everyone to like me. I'm a big girl. But I've been trying to figure you out for years. Sure, I'm not close with anyone here, but no one else seems to actively dislike me except for you. Why?"

Something like guilt flashes in Noelle's eyes. She finishes spraying down her surface and follows my lead, rounding the island and leaning back, across from me. There are only a few feet separating us in this position, and I can smell the sweet, spicy scent of her even more than I usually can.

"I don't suppose telling you it's not actually about you would be enough to get you to stop wondering?" she asks, sighing when I shake my head.

Truthfully, I'm surprised she's not straight-up shutting me down.

"Fine. I recognize that this is irrational and petty, but you stole my dream," she says, finally, and I'm no less confused.

"I stole your dream?"

"Yeah. You couldn't have known, but I've dreamed of opening the first bakery in Wintermore since I moved here. I was supposed to do it after college, but I couldn't because Felix couldn't get his shit together, and I had to work at the toy store. Then you came along and did it first." She sounds resigned, but her cheeks turn pink, like she's embarrassed.

It makes sense. Of course she resents me being here. Sure, I couldn't have known, but to put your dreams on hold for someone else is bad enough, let alone someone swooping in and stealing that dream from right under your feet before you get the chance to make it happen. I'd be pissed off too.

"I'm sorry," I say, and Noelle shrugs.

"Not your fault."

"No, but it's still shit. For what it's worth, Noelle, I might have done it first, but you did it better."

She scoffs, but I step forward, and it dies on her tongue.

"I'm serious. I'm proud of *Épices et Sucré*, and I've done better than I could've hoped, but you've made something amazing here. And with a lot less experience. It's incredible."

"Thanks," she replies, looking unconvinced.

"You don't believe me?"

"It's not… Okay, yes, the bakery has done well. But how much of that is because of me and how much of it is because of who my family is?" Bitterness seeps out of her, her brows pinching together, but she quickly recovers. "That makes me sound ungrateful, and I'm not, I just—"

"Noelle. You don't have to explain yourself. You can be grateful for the support and frustrated that it's smothering," I point out gently.

"I never said smothering."

"You didn't have to. I live and work across the street from you. I've been watching you for months, and I can see the toll it's taken on you."

The edges of Noelle's lips lift in a soft smile. "You've been watching me, huh?"

Shit. "Uh, I mean, I… Fuck. I don't suppose you can pretend I didn't say that?"

"Nope." Noelle pushes off the island and heads toward my pile of mess by the sink. "But I won't ask any follow-up questions. Come on—let's tackle this chaos and get out of here."

"You don't have to help," I say, quickly rushing over.

"I don't mind." She grabs the stack of mixing bowls and a spatula to scrape out the remnants. "For the record, I don't dislike you as much as I did a few weeks ago. Though you probably guessed that from the kiss."

"I figured."

We're both quiet as we clean. She scrapes and I sort the mess into piles: trash, rinse for the dishwasher, hand wash, put away. I wash, and she puts things away and rinses. All things considered, we get through it quickly.

Noelle closes the dishwasher, turns it on, and clears her throat, looking over her shoulder at me. "Back to what started this whole conversation: I'm sorry for kissing you, and it won't happen again. It was inappropriate."

Right. I try not to let the disappointment I have no business feeling show as I answer, "Of course. You're right. I'm a lot older than you."

I drain the sink and dry my hands on my apron. When I look up, Noelle is looking at me strangely.

"What?"

"That's not what I meant. We work together, and that could get messy quickly. Your age isn't an issue."

She said she looked me up on Facebook, but maybe she doesn't realize how old I actually am. "I'm almost forty-seven."

"I know."

"And you're thirty."

"Believe it or not, I knew that too."

I squint at her. "My point being, I'm old."

Noelle snorts, pulling the claw clip from her hair and clipping it to the strap of her denim overalls. I watch her lilac waves tumble down her back, momentarily dizzied by the way they catch the light.

"You're not old."

She stretches her neck, her eyes closed, and my mouth goes dry.

"I feel old." I don't mean to say it, I'm just so distracted by her that my mouth moves faster than my brain.

Noelle opens her eyes, staring at me with bright pools of blue. Whatever she sees on my face makes her pupils flare. "I guess you've got to find something to make you feel young again, then," she says, her voice low. Have I ever been so turned on by a soft, southern twang before? Definitely not.

"I guess so," I agree.

Tension stretches between us like spun sugar, delicate and friable. I swallow, and Noelle tracks the movement with her eyes, her tongue skating over her bottom lip.

"Shay?"

"Yeah?"

"Why did you match with me on Locked?"

I release a long breath. It feels like we're balancing on glass. "I was filming B-roll when you kissed me. I watched it back. And yeah, you ran away, but you hesitated at the door. It felt like it meant something. And… it was a good kiss," I answer honestly.

Noelle half-laughs, toying with her hands. "It was a good kiss," she agrees. "Maybe a little… quick."

"Maybe. I watched it back in slow-mo," I admit.

"I, uh, wouldn't be against seeing that sometime," she replies, and I might be imagining it, but I swear we're inching closer together.

"I'll text it to you," I offer.

"Thanks."

She looks down at the ground, pinching her lips together, almost like she's having a conversation with herself. Every line of her body is taut, her fists clenched at her sides.

"Noelle…?"

When she looks up, her pupils have swallowed her blue eyes.

"Fuck it."

I don't have time to ask what she means before she's in front of me, grasping my face. Her lips hover over mine, and I want to scream that she doesn't just close the fucking gap.

"I didn't ask last time. I should've asked. Can I kiss you? *Please.*" The last word falls from her tongue with a groan, and I don't bother answering her, cutting her off by pressing my lips to hers, because I need to taste her plea.

She gasps, but wastes no time pulling me into her. I feel a soft tug as she pulls the hair tie from my hair, and my ponytail falls down. Noelle wraps my hair around her fingers, running her tongue across the seam of my lips until they fall apart with a moan for her.

Her tongue slips into my mouth, tentatively teasing mine as she walks me backward until my back hits the island. She tastes even better than I imagined—like cinnamon and ginger and nutmeg and coffee. Simple flavors, but they're like heaven on her tongue. I could spend years trying to replicate the taste in a cake or a cookie, but I know it would never be quite right because it would be missing *her*.

She pulls back to inhale a long breath, her gaze searching my face. Her cheeks are flushed a perfect rosy pink, her hair sticking up at all angles from where my hands find purchase.

Noelle brushes her thumb across the apple of my cheek. "God damn. Look at you. You're so fucking gorgeous."

I don't remember the last time someone looked at me with so much fire in their eyes. Her expression is dazzling, knocking the breath from my lungs.

"Shay…" She drags my name out, long and slow, shaking her head softly. "I want to touch you. I need to touch you."

"Okay," I answer, even though she never asked me a question.

"I guess you've got to find something to make you feel young again." She has no idea what she does to me.

"Are you sure?" she asks, eyeing me with uncertainty. "I'm aware that I've been a complete asshole to you for years and—"

"Noelle, it's okay. I understand. And you've been sweet to me lately."

"True, but I've still been plenty spicy, too," she replies, and the guilt on her face makes me step closer to her.

"I want *you*, Noelle. Spicy *or* sweet."

Her pupils flare, and I feel the giddy nervous rush I haven't felt since long before I met Philippe as Noelle slips her hands around my body to undo the knot holding my apron together. She tosses it to the side before looking back over her shoulder at the door.

"The polite thing to do would be to take you upstairs to my apartment," she muses, turning back to me with a mischievous glint in her eyes, "but I'm feeling about as polite as I am patient right about now, so…"

She grips my hips and lifts me with seemingly zero effort until I'm perched on the edge of the island. I squeak in surprise, but it melts into a whimper as she spreads my legs and steps between them, running her palms over my thighs, and brushing my neck with her nose.

Noelle peppers kisses across my collarbone, her hands roaming over my body. She presses her hand against my ribcage and looks up at me. "Your heart's going a mile a minute. You okay?"

I nod, but my head doesn't feel like my own. "Yeah, I—" My voice is so scratchy, I pause to clear my throat. "Sorry. I haven't done this in a while. Been with a woman—or anyone."

"Don't apologize," she says softly. Her fingers are gentle as she toys with my locket. "How long's a while?"

"I haven't been with anyone since my divorce a few years ago, but I haven't been with a woman in… God, like twenty-something years."

Noelle smiles, the sight of it making my stomach flutter.

"Well, the good news is that things haven't changed all that much in twenty years." She moves her fingers over my skin, cupping my breast and pressing her thumb against my nipple. Even through my shirt and my bra, it feels incredible. "It still feels good here,"—she drags a single finger over the denim between my legs, and I almost jump out of my skin—"and here."

A curse spills from me as she moves both hands under my shirt. Her cool fingers dance against my flaming skin, and I jump, accidentally kneeing her. Fuck, I'm getting this all wrong.

"Shit, sorry, I—"

"Shay," she says, and it sounds almost like a gentle scold. She pulls my T-shirt up over my head and discards it somewhere off to the side. "Relax, and let me make this good for you, sweetheart," she murmurs.

And I wouldn't say no to that even if I could.

16
SHAY

Noelle takes a step back, like she's trying to take in the full picture of me. She's still close enough to touch me, though, and she reaches out, running her finger over the tattoo that covers my ribs.

"This is pretty," she says, tracing the edges of the little mouse holding a bunch of forget-me-nots. "For Georgie?"

It's such a small thing. "Georgie," not "your sister." Her identity is so often stripped away, even years after her death, and it feels nice to have Noelle acknowledge her.

"Yeah. Our dad called us his three little mice growing up, and these were her favorite flowers. Nico has the same tattoo on his arm."

Noelle leans in and presses her lips against the flowers. "It's a beautiful way to honor her."

Most people get awkward and dance around the subject of my dead sister, but Noelle moves on seamlessly, dragging her lips over my skin, kissing every freckle, every stretch mark. She unbuttons my jeans, pushing the band down, and kisses the indents left behind.

It's soft and tender—relaxing. Every brush across my skin leaves behind warmth, like a sunbeam shining on me. I'm so focused on the trajectory of her mouth that I don't notice her wiggling my jeans down my hips, my body lifting automatically to help her, until I feel the cool granite against my bare thighs.

I hiss, and Noelle looks up at me with a wicked smile. Up at me because, without me noticing, she kneeled between my legs. I wouldn't be tall enough to touch her from this angle, but she certainly is. She slowly takes off my boots, then pulls my jeans off, my socks. She makes her way up my legs, one kiss after another, alternating left and right.

When she reaches my thighs, she runs her nose along the inside of my right thigh with a sigh. She presses a kiss to the top, her fingers digging into my skin, like she's branding me *mine*.

She says something, but my mind is hazy and her words are muffled because her mouth is pressed against my thigh.

"Huh?"

"Can I take these off? Please," she begs, hooking her thumbs in the waistband of my basic black underwear. I should've chosen something sexier this morning; they don't even match my pale pink lacy bra. But how could I have known that this is how the day would go?

I nod, but Noelle shakes her head.

"I want to hear you say it."

Jesus. Her voice is low and goes straight to my head, curling around me like smoke.

"Please take them off. Do whatever you want to me. I just need you to touch me." My voice doesn't sound like my own. Have I ever sounded so desperate? I'm not sure I've ever *been* so desperate.

Whatever I sound like, I can tell Noelle likes it by the way her fingers twitch against me.

It's been a long time since anyone has seen me bare, and I might feel self-conscious if she weren't looking at me like a wonder of the world as she pulls my underwear down. Noelle's eyes widen as she gets her eyes on me, her lips parting.

"I can't believe I wasted so much time not liking you, when I could've had your beautiful pussy all over my face," she says, shaking her head.

I don't have time to process the words—she leans in and runs her tongue over my clit. It's not a slow build of pleasure; it's an explosion. Fireworks burst inside me in quick succession, and I fist my hand in Noelle's hair as she lavishes me with her tongue.

"Fuck, fuck, fuck," I cry, wrapping my legs around her head. I'm trapping her, but too lost in the sensation of it all to do anything about it. And Noelle doesn't seem to mind. She alternates flicking her tongue, pressing it hard against me, then closing her lips around my clit and sucking. She moves from soft and gentle to desperate and messy and back again, over and over, until I'm practically fucking her face because I can't stop myself from moving.

She sits back on her knees, pressing her thumb to my clit in place of her tongue. The change in sensation has me slamming my hand down on the island, trying to stay upright, because I don't want to miss a second of this.

"Do I get to touch you now?" I ask as she catches her breath.

Noelle's answer is a breathy laugh. "I'm nowhere near done with you, sweetheart."

Sweetheart. That's the second time she's called me that.

I've never been one for pet names. As a kid, I dreamed of having a nickname—I was the only one of my siblings without a name that could be shortened. Nicolas has always been Nico, and Georgina was always Georgie. But I was just Shay. I've liked my name from some tongues more than others, and it's pretty when Noelle says it, but I might like "sweetheart" even more.

"Here's what's going to happen: I'm going to make you come, and we're both going to enjoy it. Then I'm going to take you upstairs, we'll order dinner, eat, *then* you can touch me, I'm going to make you come again, and we're both going to enjoy it. Sound good?"

So good. "Mhmm. But I need to feed my cat before we go upstairs."

Noelle frowns. "You have a cat?"

"Not really. Kind of. It's complicated."

She looks no less confused, but shrugs. "Alright. Let's just go to your place."

"That works."

"Great. Can I make you come now?"

Jesus. My breath catches in my throat. "Have at it."

Noelle's eyes light up.

She teases my entrance with a finger. "This okay?"

"Yeah."

Slowly, she slides one finger inside me, and my head falls back. She curls her finger, massaging gently, while her thumb puts pressure on my clit. It's been so long since I had any part of someone else inside me, and longer since it felt this good. I rock my hips to the motion of her finger, gasping when she pulls out and pushes two inside.

"Fuck, baby," I cry when she presses them against my G-spot, and she goes still for a moment.

Shit. I didn't mean to call her baby. I open my mouth to apologize, but stop when my gaze follows me. Her jaw is slack, her eyes practically black, and I only have a second to clock the lust in her expression before she's on me.

Gone is the gentle Noelle of thirty seconds ago; she catches my clit between her lips and sucks hard while rolling her fingers roughly inside me. My whole body feels like it's on fire, engulfed in flames, with ginger-scented smoke choking the air from my lungs.

Without thinking, I knot my hands in Noelle's lilac hair, and though I try not to pull, I fail miserably when she moans against me. I swear I can feel the sound in the marrow of my bones, like a zap of electricity tipping my world off its axis and sending me tumbling into beautiful oblivion that's somehow everything and nothing at all.

I fall off the cliff's edge, my mouth open in a silent scream as the orgasm ripples through me, wave after wave of overwhelming pleasure. And Noelle eats it up. Literally. If anything, my orgasm pushes her to devour me even more intensely, her tongue lavishing me like she's scared to miss a spot. I can't hear her over the blood pounding in my ears, but I can feel the vibrations as she groans against me.

Hours pass—or that's what it feels like anyway. It's only one orgasm, but Noelle drags it out beyond any I've ever had before, until my bones feel like jelly.

She pulls back, and it takes a second for my hazy vision to focus.

Her face is glistening. "That was quite the appetizer," Noelle says, licking her lips.

I almost come again at the sight. I'm fucking spent, but desperate to get her in my bed—desperate to get my hands on her. "My apartment." It's a struggle to get the words out because I still haven't caught my breath, but if the grin that lights Noelle's face is anything to go by, she likes seeing what she's done to me.

"Your place," she agrees.

She helps me down, frowning as she hands me my clothes. I've never regretted my choice of pants as much as I do trying to wriggle into jeans when I'm so fucked.

Noelle tuts. "What a waste, considering I'm taking those off you again the second we get in the door."

"What about the takeout?"

"They can leave it at the door," Noelle says, grabbing her bag. "Do you have everything?"

Almost certainly not, I think, as I look around the kitchen. I feel like my head is full of cotton balls.

"I have no idea," I admit. "I think you fried my brain."

Noelle laughs, the sound soft and twinkly like jingle bells. Fitting.

"Keys?" she prompts.

I pat my jeans pocket and nod.

"Purse?"

I pick it up from where I unceremoniously dumped it on the floor this morning.

"Phone?"

I grab it from the counter, both relieved and a little disappointed that I wasn't filming B-roll. I wouldn't mind having that to watch back in slow motion. I say as much as Noelle leads me out of the kitchen, locking the door behind us.

"Do you always watch porn in slow-mo?" she questions, drawing a laugh that takes more energy than I realize I have from me.

"Can you do that?"

She shrugs. "Probably. Sometimes I watch at double speed when I'm in a rush."

I follow her across the street, gaping at her back. "Are you serious? Tell me you're messing with me."

"I'm a busy girl!"

"That's the saddest thing I've ever heard," I say, shaking my head in disbelief.

We climb the stairs to my apartment, and Cat appears, as always, like he's just been waiting for me. He has access to my apartment when I'm gone—I always leave a small window open, and he can access it via the patio—and I know he hangs out on my couch and my bed based on the indents he leaves. Sometimes, I think he greets me at the door just to make me feel guilty for leaving him all day.

Not that he seems all that excited to see *me* this evening. He stops short, chirping at the sight of Noelle, and promptly flops over on her feet.

"Oh my god!" she squeals, practically tossing her bag aside in favor of picking him up. "Look at you, sweet baby. What's your name?"

I pick up her bag and shoulder it as I unlock the apartment door. "I don't know his name, so I just call him Cat," I explain, and she removes her face from Cat's belly—where she appears to be blowing raspberries—to stare at me with a horrified expression.

"And that's the saddest thing *I've* ever heard. What the hell, Shay? Name your cat!"

"He's not actually my cat. He just showed up and moved in one day."

I pour his food into his bowl, and he meows until Noelle lets him down. You'd think he'd never been fed.

"You just described owning a cat," Noelle says, smiling fondly at Cat. "Sounds like he chose you to be his mom."

Maybe she's right. Not just about naming him—he deserves something a little more permanent. And maybe I could stop referring to him as "not actually my cat." If he wants to be my cat, I could be his human, I suppose.

"Moving on from Cat," I say, leaning against the kitchen counter and taking in Noelle in my space. I realize, with a jolt, that she's the first person I've had in here since I've moved in. And she... Fuck, she fits well. I swallow. "So, what was it you said about ordering food and me getting to touch you?"

17

NOELLE

My imagination didn't do her justice.

She tastes like a lemon drop, sweet and sour, and she goes straight to my head faster than any shot ever has. I think I could spend hours just kissing her and be perfectly content. We haven't even made it to her bed yet, because I pushed her against her bedroom door the second it was closed. She puts her whole body into the kiss, pressing it against me. Her fingers rake down my back, and she gasps as my tongue dances with hers.

I step back, tugging her with me. Her cheeks are flushed, her gray eyes hazy. Stopping as the back of my legs hit the edge of the bed, I pull my sweater over my head and throw it aside. I'm wearing a tight crop top under it, but Shay's eyes widen. She swallows, like the gravity of everything is hitting her all at once.

"Still with me, sweetheart?"

She nods, slowly dragging her gaze up from my exposed midriff. "Yeah. It's just, it's been a while. What if I…" She trails off, biting her lip nervously.

I clasp both her hands with mine, pulling them toward me.

"You don't need to worry about that. I think I could come just from kissing you."

"But I want to do more than that."

"Oh, we're going to," I tell her. I place her hands on the waistband of my pants, and her fingers take over, unclasping my belt. She draws it out of my belt loops torturously slowly, and I feel every bit of the friction as it slides around my waist.

Shay drops it to the floor and moves onto my button next, then my zipper. I expect her to just push my pants down, but she sinks to the floor with them, looking up at me, and sending my heart haywire.

She kisses her way up my body, every stamp of her lips so light that it feels like a feather tickling my skin. She hooks her fingers in the band of my crop top, and I raise my arms so she can tug it off. I have to close my eyes and take a deep breath at the soft curse that falls from her lips, the sound coursing down my body, fluttering over my skin, like an autumn leaf.

Her fingers are trembling as she toys with my bra clasp, trying to undo it. I lean down, pressing my forehead against hers, and feel her body relax into me.

She undoes the clasp, and I shrug out of my bra. I can't look away as she steps back, taking me in. Shay's lips part, her gray eyes going impossibly dark as she lets her gaze traverse every inch of my body. I keep my eyes on her as I push my underwear down and step out of it. The breath rushes out of her.

I kneel on the bed, shuffling backward so I can watch as she undresses—quickly, like she wants to close the distance between us as soon as she can. And close it she does; the second her clothes are on the floor, Shay is crawling on the bed toward me, her expression ravenous.

She sits up on her knees when she reaches me, steadying herself by grasping my waist. Her thumbs press lightly into my hips, and the feel of her draws my body in closer to her.

I'm a second from begging her to touch me when she drags her hands up my torso and brushes her thumbs over my nipples. My head falls back, a groan spilling from me. The ends of my hair tickle my lower back as my body bows toward her.

Shay's touch is hesitant, like she's overthinking every shift of her fingers over before she moves them. My brain feels one step ahead of every movement, and something about the anticipation drives me wild. Until she does something completely unexpected and ducks her head, circling one of my nipples with her tongue.

I clench my fists as the heat of her mouth consumes me. Each flick of her tongue sends a ripple of pleasure through me, like little pinpricks of electricity hitting me from all angles. I sink my fingers into her hair and gasp as she draws my nipple between her lips.

"Fuck, sweetheart. That feels so good."

"You feel good," she murmurs, kissing the spot between my breasts before sweeping her tongue over my other nipple.

With one hand, she grips my thigh; the other traverses the shape of me, settling between my legs. I feel her take a deep breath before she draws her finger through my lips, pressing the tip against my clit.

I'm so goddamn sensitive that I cry out, my hips pressing into her of their own accord. My cry spurs her on, and she adds a second finger, rolling my clit between them—slow but building.

"Oh," I whimper, rocking against her hand. I cup her chin, pulling her face up and bending down so I can kiss her. I savor every second of the kiss, her tongue dancing against mine until we have no choice but to break apart to catch our breath.

Shay places her free hand flat on my chest and nudges me back.

"Lie down."

I do as I'm told, lying back on her silky bedding until my head is nestled against her pillow. I turn to the side, overwhelmed by the sweet, summery scent of her. It's all too easy to imagine her lying here, thinking about our kiss, watching it back in slow motion.

But once again, my imagination has nothing on the real thing.

In my head, Shay is a hazy glow. In reality, kneeling between my thighs, licking her lips as she stares down at my naked body, she's blinding.

"Will you tell me if it's not good?" she asks, like there's any possibility here that I'm not going to explode the second she puts her mouth on me.

"Shay, sweetheart, I'm about to come just from how you're looking at me. You have nothing to worry about."

She chuckles, but I see the tension in the way she has her shoulders set.

"Come here," I say, beckoning her with my index finger.

Shay leans over me, and I press a gentle kiss to her lips, cupping her face. A soft fall breeze makes her sheer curtains flutter, bathing her in the warm golden hour glow. The air swirls around her, and I swear the scent of her is going to be permanently embedded in my brain after this.

"Of course I'll tell you, but I promise you don't need to worry. Everything you do feels amazing."

"Yeah?" she whispers against my mouth.

"Did you not feel how fucking soaked I am? That's all because of you, sweetheart. All for you."

Her eyes widen, and she bites her lip before sitting back so she's hovering right between my legs. Shay strokes her finger through my center, and I whimper.

"For me, huh?" she asks, bringing her finger to her mouth and sucking it between her lips. She groans, and I can't help but tighten my legs around her, like I'm drawing her in closer to me.

Shay doesn't seem to mind; she leans over, parting me and swallowing as she stares down at my pussy.

I think I actually black out for a second at the first pass of her tongue over my clit, and when I come to, my back is arched off the bed, and my legs are on her shoulders. She teases me, her tongue gentle as she flicks the tip against me, then she closes her lips around my clit. I'm already teetering on a tightrope, seconds from flying, when Shay presses one finger inside me. Her hands are small, delicate, and she feels so fucking good inside me when she curls her finger, stroking me until I find myself tightening around her.

My breaths come hard and fast and loud, incoherent mumblings of her name, and *please* and *fuck* tumbling from me as I tumble off the edge, spiraling into a kaleidoscope of colors and sensations. And all it seems to do is boost Shay's confidence as she licks me faster, like she wants this to last as long as possible. I feel her everywhere, spreading fire through my veins as I fall to pieces for her.

And when I taste myself on her tongue when she kisses me after a moment, when I listen to her humming ABBA as she does her skincare an hour later, when I watch her fall asleep, a peaceful smile on her face, and all I can think about is how I'd like to slot her into every aspect of my life…

Yeah, my imagination didn't prepare me for this at all. I'm so fucked.

18
SHAY

Noelle is gone when I wake up the next morning. Six a.m., and the side of the bed she slept in is stone cold. I know she slept here—I wake up a lot through the night, and I saw her sleeping soundly, Cat curled up against her back. She's probably used to waking up early for work, but I can't pretend it doesn't feel a little like she snuck out in the dead of night. Without even leaving a note on the pillow. Do people even do that outside of movies?

It's stupid. This was just a hookup. Casual. A one-time thing… I think. We didn't talk about it, but she told me she didn't have time to date before our meeting with the mayor, so I know it's not more than sex. Shit, my brain is fried.

I feed Cat and scratch between his ears until he's a happy little ball of fluff and purrs, before stretching and heading into the kitchen to feed myself. I stop dead: there's a plate covered in aluminum foil, and a note on the counter.

My curiosity gets the better of me, and I take off the foil before opening the note, finding a breakfast sandwich, bursting with what looks like mushrooms and some kind of cheese, clearly handmade. On a Christmas plate. She brought this from home, which means…

She left and brought me back breakfast. What the hell does that mean?

I unfold the note, laughing when I see it's just cooking instructions. Of course it is.

My coffee machine is prepped, too, a cup sitting beside it and all. She really did think of everything, and I have no idea what to make of it.

I follow Noelle's instructions to a T, and before long, my apartment smells buttery and garlicky. With my coffee, breakfast sandwich, and Cat on my heels, I sit on the balcony to enjoy it all. The sun is a blur of orange on the horizon, but Wintermore's main street is bustling. This is always a busy time of day, since a lot of residents leave town early to beat the traffic for their 9-to-5s in Jackson, or make it to the early morning shuttles that run to the nearby mountain resorts. The job market in Wintermore itself is lacking, unless you own or work for a local business.

Since the movie people arrived in town, though, the mornings have been nothing short of chaos. I'm not sure where they're squeezing all these people into such a small town, but from my perch, I can see no less than thirty crew members milling around, looking down at their phones and clutching coffee cups from The Enchanted Bakery or The Frosty Bean. There's something oddly relaxing about sitting up here, finishing off Noelle's breakfast sandwich—delicious, naturally—and looking down at everything happening with nowhere to be.

Truthfully, with the café side of *Épices et Sucré* being closed, I've gotten ahead on my custom orders, and my workload has dwindled to almost nothing—besides the baking Noelle and I are doing for the movie. I can't pretend I'm not enjoying the reprieve a little, but mostly I'm enjoying just working with another person again. Sure, I have Gracie around most of the time, but we work in different rooms.

I would offer to help at The Enchanted Workshop if I didn't think Noelle would find a shallow grave for me somewhere, so

I've been trying to get ahead on the movie baking as much as I can while things are quiet, to take some of the pressure off.

I've had time to get ahead on my admin stuff, make tons of social media content, and, apparently, time to have sex with a woman almost seventeen years younger than me. I have one week of forty-six left, and I'm going out with a bang, it seems.

Speaking of making changes, Cat curls up against me, kneading my hip with his little paws, purring away.

"So," I begin, scratching his chin, "I think we need to talk."

"Meow."

It's something.

"Do you want to live here? Like for real."

"Meow."

"And do you want me to be your mom?"

His answering "meow" is more of a yawn, but I'll take it.

"Okay, well, I'll go to the pet store this weekend and get you more stuff, and I'll make an appointment for the V-E-T to get you checked over." I spell it out, on the off chance he knows the word, and with the understanding that I'm having a seemingly two-way conversation with a cat, and I'm probably losing my mind.

"I should probably give you a real name, huh?"

I look him over. He's mostly black, with little tufts of chocolate brown peppered throughout his smooth coat, and a single white patch on one paw. He's purring contentedly, curled up like a burned croissant…

"Croissant," I say, and he cracks one orange eye, meowing in agreement. "Alright. Croissant it is—but the proper pronunciation. You tell me if anyone pronounces it like 'crah-sawnt,' okay?"

He doesn't reply. Because he's a cat, and I, once again, am losing my mind.

I really have to get out more.

My morning passes in bowl after bowl of batter, frosting, and ganache, as I work in the basement kitchen.

Thinking about Noelle.

Wondering what Noelle is doing.

Assuming Noelle regrets everything.

Wondering what to expect from Noelle.

Hearing Noelle call me sweetheart.

Remembering how Noelle tastes.

Remembering how Noelle sounds when she comes.

It can all be summed up as spiraling about Noelle. And it doesn't make the day pass any faster. She turns up a couple of hours after lunch, and I do a wonderful job of pretending like I haven't been on edge all day.

And by that, I mean I spot her and immediately knock an entire bowl of lemon curd over with my elbow. I'm not proud of the curse that slips out of my mouth.

Noelle stops in her tracks, staring wide-eyed as the ocean of sticky yellow curd floods over the island and spills onto the floor beyond.

"Well, then." She moves slowly across the kitchen, dodging the curd as she comes closer. "You know, most people are a little less frazzled the day after multiple orgasms." She stops at the edge of the island and swipes her finger through the lemon puddle, bringing it to her lips and groaning. "Fuck, that's good."

I wouldn't be surprised if I passed out at this point. I'm almost forty-seven years old. What business do I have getting this flustered over someone?

I cover my face with my hands and sigh; they smell like lemon. "I'm sorry for the mess. I'll clean it—"

"Shay." Soft fingers close around my wrists, and Noelle tugs my hands away. She eyes me with concern. "It's not a big deal. Breathe for a second. I'll clean it up."

"But it's my mess. I don't—"

She levels me with a singular raised eyebrow that stops the protest on my tongue.

I wipe the curd from the island while she mops it off the floor. It doesn't take long, and she seems comfortable working in silence. Meanwhile, my head is screaming.

When she finally looks up, she narrows her eyes. "What's going on with you? Are you upset about... Do you regret last night?"

What I should do, to wipe the crestfallen expression off her face, is assure her that no, I don't regret last night. In fact, I'm pretty sure it's the best sex I've ever had, and I'm more confused than ever because I want to do it again. I don't know what that means for me, for us.

Instead, I blurt out, "I named the cat. And I made him a vet appointment. You're right—he's mine, or I'm his, or however it works."

Noelle blinks in surprise, her eyes softening. "Good. What did you name him?"

"Croissant."

"Excellent choice." She leans on the island, her face a mere two feet from mine. "Excellent pronunciation. Do you speak French?"

"Yeah. Not perfectly, but well enough. Do you?"

She shakes her head. "Always wanted to, but I've never had the patience for languages. French is so fucking hot, though. Tell me something sexy." Her eyes twinkle, and it calms me. *She calms me.*

I think for a moment before settling on, *"J'ai passée une*

incroyable soirée. Tu es toujours magnifique, mais espécialement quand tu t'effondres pour moi."

Noelle's lips part. Her pupils dilate, and her cheeks burn maroon. Interesting.

"I have no idea what you just said, but don't tell me. It sounded hot. *You* sound hot."

She leans in closer and kisses me, breathing me in with a happy-sounding sigh. When she pulls back, she licks her lips, and I have to look away.

"Noelle."

"Hmm?"

"I don't think I can do this." I sound as panicked as I feel, and a lot less cool than I'd like to.

"Oh. Okay…"

Shit. She sounds hurt.

"I just feel really old right now," I admit, still refusing to look at her.

Which she clearly notices, because she rounds the island until she's standing in front of me.

"Talk to me. Old how?"

"Old like… Shit, I don't know. I haven't done casual sex in a long time. I don't know if last night was a one-time thing, or if you want to do it again, or… Hell, whatever this is, I'm flying pretty blind right now, and I feel like I'm going to fall flat on my face, because I don't know what's going on. And I know it's probably uncool of me to be acting like this literally one day after we slept together, but I've been thinking about you all day, and I—"

She cuts me off with another kiss. It's soft, until it's not, and I'm not sure which of us takes it up a notch. But I sure as hell don't mind it when she backs me against the kitchen counter and bites down on my lip. She kisses her way across my jaw and down my throat, before pressing her forehead against mine.

For a moment, we both just breathe each other in.

"If it makes you feel better, I've been thinking about you all day, too. And I don't care if you're not cool—I'm not either," she adds with a soft chuckle, but it sounds almost strained. I can't figure out her expression, a little forced—almost too level.

She steps back enough that she can look at me, but keeps her arms locked on either side of me. When Philippe used to cage me like this, I felt claustrophobic, but Noelle feels like fresh air.

"You're not old, sweetheart. Certainly not because you don't know what you're doing here. I don't either." Noelle toys with her lip, and I wish I were instead. "I would like to do it again. A lot, actually. We can just go with the flow and figure out what casual sex looks like for us."

"Go with the flow…" I repeat slowly. "Yeah, totally, I can go with the flow. Will you like, tell me if I'm doing it wrong? Or anything wrong. Actually, ignore me. I sound needy."

"Shay." Her lips lift in an amused smile, and she brushes my hair back from my face. "Yes, I'll tell you. But you're not going to do anything wrong. We're figuring it out together, and I've got you. Okay?"

"Okay," I whisper, because her lips are creeping closer to mine, and it's all I can do to remember how to breathe. She makes me feel out-of-my-mind drunk.

Noelle surprises me by kissing, not my lips, but the tip of my nose. "Who would have thought the person who works in complete and utter chaos would be so frazzled by the idea of going with the flow?"

"I like the chaos, because I like putting it back in order," I explain. "And it's not the going with the flow that frazzles me. It's you."

"I'm going to take that as a compliment."

"It is, *mon délice*," I say, my blood warming when she sucks in a breath at the French term of endearment.

"I'm torn between wanting to know what that means and not, because the mystery is almost sexier."

I mime zipping my lips, and she laughs.

"Where do we start? With the whole going with the flow thing?" I ask.

She looks over her shoulder and snorts. "With a new batch of lemon curd, I think."

19

NOELLE

In my humble opinion, I'm doing a great job of pretending like I know what I'm doing, but I really, *really* don't.

As far as everyone else is concerned, I'm thriving at The Enchanted Bakery. As far as everyone else is concerned, I'm living the goddamn dream. And as far as Shay is concerned, I'm totally cool and chill about "going with the flow," whatever the fuck that means.

In reality, I'm floundering.

I'm not even sure why I said it, beyond the fact that *she* was clearly panicking, and we couldn't both do it. There's a surprisingly loud part of me that can't bear the thought of a woman I hated less than a week ago being upset about literally anything. I don't know why, and I don't know how, but Shay's well-being has become somewhat of a priority for me over the past few days, and I'm avoiding unpacking what that means.

She looks good in my apartment. I'm avoiding unpacking what that means, too.

Because Shay called this casual sex. And I… Fuck, I woke up this morning and thought about bringing her to my parents' house for Christmas. Not exactly casual.

She seemed so anxious, though, so if she wants casual, I can do casual. I guess.

I watch her from the kitchen, pretending to focus on the

components of the cocktails I offered to make us—pumpkin spice old-fashioneds. Shay is taking in every detail, her eyes missing nothing as she wanders around my living room. There's admittedly not much to it; I don't spend a lot of time here. When I finally moved out of my parents' house, I more or less copy and pasted my bedroom into this apartment, just spread out a little more.

My taste in decor hasn't ever changed much. I was born into a Christmas family, and I feel most at home surrounded by twinkling lights, tinsel, and the life-size nutcracker in the corner that scares Sunny every time Rora brings her over here. I may have to get rid of that, actually.

"Do you keep this up all year?" Shay asks, pointing to the Christmas tree in the corner as I pop pumpkin-shaped ice cubes made with pumpkin puree out of the silicone mold.

"Yeah, but I get a real tree closer to Christmas, too." Artificial trees are a necessity if you keep them up year-round, like my family does, but I love the smell of a real fir tree.

"You should decorate it for each season. A Halloween tree would be cute," Shay says as I cross the room.

I press the old-fashioned into her hand with a wry laugh. "Next year, maybe."

Shay brings the glass to her lips, her eyes closing as she sips the drink and lets out a soft sigh. "God, that's good."

A drop runs down her lip, and I don't hesitate to bring my thumb to her chin, catching the drop. Shay flicks her tongue out, licking the drop from my thumb, and my knees almost buckle.

"I like it," she says after pressing a kiss to the tip of my thumb.

"The drink?"

"That too, but I meant your apartment. It feels like you."

"A Christmas tree in September will do that," I point out, but she shakes her head.

"It's not that. It's… warm. Cozy. A little intimidating, if I'm being honest." She's smiling when she says it, so I don't worry too much.

"You find me intimidating?"

"I find you terrifying, *mon délice.*"

There she goes again with the French. I suddenly regret taking Spanish in high school. I *could* look it up, but something about the mystery, not knowing what she's saying, is so much hotter than knowing.

"Everything about this is terrifying. But I like it. I think," she continues, sounding decidedly less confident than when she started speaking. "I'm just nervous, I guess. I've wanted us to be friends for a long time, you know? We have so much in common, and I thought maybe if we were working together, we'd have coffee or something. I didn't expect this. I like it, don't get me wrong. Shit, this is all coming out wrong."

It's not coming out wrong. I understand her. I don't like it, but I get it.

Friends. Who sleep together, yeah, but… friends. At least she said something before I told her that I haven't just been thinking about last night all day—I've been thinking about taking her on dates, braving the treacherous road up to Rora's cabin and hiding out for a few days together, matching Christmas sweaters. So maybe I let my crush get ahead of me a little. It happens. It's fine.

I thread my fingers through hers, tugging her to the couch as quickly as her uncertainty tugs at my heartstrings. We put our drinks down on matching gingerbread woman coasters, and Shay bites her lip as I rub my thumb over the back of her hand.

"Sweetheart, I don't want you feeling uncomfortable. This is…" I sigh, trying to find the words. "At the start of this week, I thought I didn't like you. And now you're sitting on my couch, and I'm sad that you're going to have to leave to feed Croissant in a couple of hours." A smile flits around her mouth. "I guess what

I'm trying to say is that I'm just as surprised by all this as you are." And confused. So fucking confused. "I would love to be… friends." *Casual,* I remind myself. She wants things casual.

God, I really hate that word all of a sudden.

Shay pulls her hand from mine, and I frown at the absence of her. She rubs her face, groaning. "I'm sorry. I know I said earlier that I could go with the flow, and I *will*, it just might take me a while to adjust. Trying to get out of my own head is harder than I expected."

I consider her—the flare of panic in her gray eyes, the smudge of purple below them, the bite mark on her lip—and swallow. "What is it that you're getting stuck on—my age? Or is it… Is it because I'm a woman?"

I've been operating under the assumption that Shay is comfortable with her sexuality, since she was openly looking for women on Locked, but I've never actually asked.

"What?" Shay's eyes widen a fraction. "No, of course…" She trails off, wincing. "Shit. No, it's not that. But it's not *not* that… God, not to sound like a cliché, but it's not you, it's me. I'm sorry, I—"

I interrupt her spiraling, saying her name softly, and she looks at me, guilt flooding her face.

"I'm not taking this personally, I promise. I just want to know where you're at, and what I can do to make it easier."

Shay takes a deep breath. "Your age is an issue, yeah. I know you're an adult and old enough to know what you want, but I've never been… attracted to someone so much younger than me, and I'm processing. Like, I know your parents. I see them around, and I can't imagine they'd be okay with you sleeping with someone so much older than you."

I can't stop myself from snorting. It's not an unreasonable concern, but in our family… Not a problem. "You know, my parents practically raised Rora. They consider her theirs as much as me and Felix, and she fell in love and had a baby with my uncle. My parents are technically Sunny's aunt and uncle, but they go by grandma and grandpa. And Uncle Henry is nineteen years older than Rora, so I don't think my family would bat an eye at this."

Shay looks momentarily stunned. "What the hell? I knew he was older, but wow. I can see why my age doesn't bother you. As for you being a woman—short answer, no. Of course it doesn't bother me. I'm not straight."

"I did realize that."

"Right," she answers, with a chuckle. "I'm bi, I guess, but I haven't let myself think about it for a long time. If we're friends now, I should tell you about Philippe, huh?"

"I want to learn whatever you want to share."

She looks down at her lap, picking her nails. "I never pictured myself with a man. Ever. My parents are good parents, but they don't like change, so I never told them I was dating women. It's not that I think they would've had an issue with it, and I did plan to tell them.

"Nico and I were going to do it together—he was seeing a guy from work and wanted to bring him home for Thanksgiving, so we were going to tell them before, but then…"

"Georgie died."

Shay's lips curve into a smile, as they always seem to when we talk about her sister, even when it's a shitty topic. I'm guessing she doesn't get to talk about her much. People get weird about death, but staying quiet about the people we lose does nothing to keep the memory of them alive.

"Exactly. Georgie died, and Nico didn't handle it well. He's always blamed himself. The second he woke and realized she was gone, he shut everyone out. He broke up with his boyfriend, and he pushed me and my parents away, and it felt like it was my responsibility to keep everything together."

I can hear the grief in her voice, and I want to wrap her up in my arms and hold her tight. And I will—when she's ready. If she wants that. Friends can comfort each other.

"That's a lot to shoulder so soon after losing your sister."

"It was," she admits. "Georgie and I did a year of college in Paris. She was obsessed with France, and I wanted to learn from the best, so it worked out well. We met Philippe while we were there—don't let his name fool you, he's from Idaho, and he changed it when he moved to France. He and Georgie worked together, and they were really close. He came back to the US just before she died, and he came to her funeral. My parents liked him, and he was the only person who would talk about Georgie with me. We were friends who were both grieving someone, and we loved each other, but we were never in love. Honestly, I don't think either of us ever thought we were, but it was what we needed at the time. What my parents needed."

"How long were you married?" I ask, almost scared to know the answer.

"Seventeen years. And I know that sounds bad. It's easy to think we wasted a good chunk of our lives together, but I don't see it as a waste, and neither does he. We enjoyed our time together. Neither of us wanted kids; we were happy having two incomes, and we liked hanging out. But he met someone else, someone he's actually in love with, and we were both perfectly happy to go our separate ways."

I like to think I could be content with something like that, but I don't think I could. I look at my parents, who have been together for four decades and still look at each other like newlyweds, and I want that. I look at Rora and my uncle Henry, building a life together, and I want that. Not the baby part of it, but the all-consuming, life-changing kind of love that completely turns your world upside down.

But I also understand why Shay wanted, needed, something

easier after having her world turned upside down in the worst possible way.

"How did your parents take the divorce?" I ask, and she shrugs.

"They were disappointed. But we're not close anymore, so it didn't sting as much as it would have once. Nico and I take turns calling them once a week, but it's hard to be close when no one will talk about anything deeper than surface level because they're too scared to talk about Georgie." There's a bitter edge to her voice that I tuck away for later.

I recognize how lucky I am to say I can't imagine not talking to my family every day. They're the first people I call when I just want to talk to someone—if I don't just show up, that is.

"Anyway," Shay continues, "I'm a lot older and less traumatized now, and I don't care if people find out I'm bi. It's more that it's been a long time since I've thought about what *I* want. Like, do I really want to be in another relationship? Do I just want to have good sex for the first time in twenty years? I know I want you, that I'm sure of, but I don't know what that looks like. And it just feels like I'm too old to be figuring any of this out, you know?"

I bring her hand to my lips and press them against her palm. "I don't know what I have to do to convince you you're not old, but I'm going to keep trying. Right now, I think the best thing for both of us to do is just… hang out. I want to keep sleeping with you, but I also don't want to push you if you don—"

"I do. I just feel a little out of my depth with it all."

I laugh at how quickly she interrupts. "How about this: we can figure out together how to make you more comfortable with it. But you have to talk to me, okay? Sex is more fun when you're honest about how you feel," I say, well aware that I'm lying through my teeth about how *I* feel.

"I can do that," Shay agrees. "And I want to get to know you, too. I wasn't kidding when I said I've wanted to be your friend for years, even if that does make me sound a little pathetic."

"It doesn't make you sound pathetic at all. I'm sorry it took me so long to get my shit together and stop being an asshole so we could be friends," I say, trying to ignore how much "friends" feels like a lead weight getting heavier and heavier in my stomach.

SHAY

She has another Christmas tree in her bedroom, but it's not the tree that catches my attention; it's the ornaments.

"I could lie and say I didn't make my bed because I was in a rush when I left yesterday morning, but I'm always in a rush, and I never make my bed, so there's no point in pretending," Noelle says, and I hear her fussing with the bed as I stare at the tree.

She notices my gaze and groans. "Right. That. I ordered an Advent calendar from a super sketchy website last year, and it was supposed to be a bunch of mini *usable* sex toy ornaments, but it ended up being just twenty-one butt plugs, a bullet vibe, and a pair of broken handcuffs—one cuff on December fifth, one on the twelfth. They don't even clip together. What a waste."

"Is that… The Grinch?" I ask, prodding a green plug that is definitely The Grinch.

"It is. I considered giving it to Rora, actually, since she hates Christmas, but she's sleeping with my uncle, so it felt too weird."

"Jesus." Because what else do I say to that?

"Yeah." Noelle draws the word out. "If I'd known I was having company, I would probably have moved the butt plug tree. And in the interest of giving you a crash course in getting to know me, let's get all of my weird decor out of the way…"

She places her hands gently on either side of me, spins me

until I'm facing her bed, then tilts my chin until I'm staring over the headboard.

It takes me a second to process what I'm seeing, and when I do… "Wow."

"I thought it would be empowering, you know?" she explains as we both take in the six strap-on harnesses secured to the wall, in almost every color of the rainbow. "I saw someone online with a similar display, and they said it inspired them to own their sexuality, but their display was a lot nicer than mine, and you're the first woman I've had in here, so… Also, the blue one kept falling off and hitting me in the middle of the night, so I just shoved it under the bed."

"I'm the first woman you've had in here?" It's not that I'm not listening to her, it's just that nothing registers after I hear that.

"Yep. I haven't exactly had a lot of time for socializing since I moved in." Noelle sits on the end of the bed with a sigh. "You probably think I'm unhinged."

"Are you kidding me?" I take a seat beside her and grab her hand. "You're making me reassess how fucking boring everyone else in my life is. You are, without a doubt, the coolest person I know, Noelle."

She quirks a smile. "Damn. You've really got to meet some new people."

"I don't want to meet anyone else. I'm here, aren't I?" I reply, nudging her foot with mine.

"Yeah." Her smile softens. "You are."

"I've never used one, you know," I say, nodding to the display.

"A strap?"

"No, a Grinch butt plug," I reply, rolling my eyes.

She laughs, a warm, honeyed sound that goes to my head more than the old-fashioned has. "Damn, I can't believe it. You totally give me Grinch butt plug vibes, sweetheart. But seriously, I like toys. I like trying new things out, but I can have plenty of fun without them if you're not into them."

"I don't really know what I'm into," I reply honestly. "But I'm open to trying whatever you think I might like. I trust you."

She sits up straighter, like she likes hearing me say I trust her. And I do.

Truthfully, I'm entirely out of my element here. I've used exactly one sex toy—a trusty rabbit I've had for longer than I'd like to admit—and my sexual history is beyond basic. With Philippe, it was once every couple of months at the most, usually on a special occasion, or when we were a little tipsy. Before Philippe, I was never with anyone long enough to get comfortable and try anything new.

Noelle makes me want to try new things, though.

"Do you have a big collection?" I ask, and she nods, beckoning me over to her nightstand.

She pulls open the bottom drawer, and I'm honestly surprised she managed to get it closed; it's so full. It's a rainbow of pink, and purple, various nude shades, and bright blue… "Are those tentacles?"

Her cheeks turn as pink as the spiral of pink silicon sitting on top of the drawer. I couldn't even begin to guess how it's used.

"Technically, it's just one tentacle. I was curious, but it's not my thing," Noelle explains. "When I'm not working, which is most of the time, or with my family, I like to just stay home, and this drawer makes for the best kind of stress relief I've got right now. It's amazing what a vibrator, whatever fantasy I'm fixating on at the moment, and thirty minutes to myself will do."

"I get that," I say, peering into the drawer. "Have you ever thought about me?" I don't mean to say it; the question slips from my tongue like it demands to be heard. But I don't regret it when Noelle's pupils flare in response.

"After I kissed you. I tried every other way to distract myself, but nothing worked. I got the notification to say you'd matched with me right as I came."

God. Why is that so hot?

"What one did you use?" I ask, looking back at the drawer.

Noelle leans down and pulls out a hot pink toy with what I think is a suction head. I've never used one, but I'm not completely naive about what's what.

"Can you show me how it works?"

"You want me to use it on you?" Noelle asks, her voice low. The little twang she has seems to be stronger when she's turned on, and it coils around me, squeezing the breath from my lungs.

I shake my head, and her eyes widen. "I want to watch you use it."

"Fuck," Noelle whispers. "Of course. Yes. But only if I get to watch you, too."

She grabs another toy from the drawer and passes it to me. The pink toy she has is bigger, with a curved handle that I suspect means it can be used internally as well as externally. The silver one she hands me has the same suction head, but it's smaller and more oval-shaped.

"I've never used suction," I say, and by the time I look up from the toy, she's already half undressed.

A wicked smile curves her lips. "Prepare to have your mind blown. Once you try suction, you can never go back." She must notice my dubious expression as I look at the toy, because she adds, "Trust me. This is one of those times where size doesn't matter."

I turn away to get undressed, folding my clothes and setting them on her dresser. I'm usually a ball things up in the corner of the room kind of person, but something about undressing in front of each other feels more intimate than it has the past two times, when I was so caught up in the moment, I didn't even consider feeling self-conscious.

Now, though, I can't help it. I wasn't kidding when I told Noelle I felt old, and my body looks exactly like what you'd expect from the body of an almost-forty-seven-year-old who never works out and spent too much time in the sun as a teenager. There's a softness to my stomach, a sagginess to my breasts that I didn't have when I was Noelle's age. I have a large scar that starts a couple inches below my belly button, curves around, and continues up my abdomen, from my emergency surgery after the accident. My grays come in faster than I can dye them; I have sunspots, and stretch marks, and all kinds of things I didn't have to think about when I was married to a man who was aging at the same time I was. A thirty-year-old is a whole other ballgame.

But when I turn around, Noelle is lying back against her pillows with an expression that can only be described as ravenous.

"The fantasy had nothing on reality," she says, shaking her head as she takes me in. "Look at you."

The reverence in her voice propels me forward until I'm sitting opposite her on the bed. I could lie beside her—it would be more comfortable—but I want to see her.

She spreads her legs, pressing the back of the toy until a hidden button glows white.

"Your turn."

It's hard not to just sit and stare, still as a statue, but I force myself to pick up the toy, inspecting it. The buttons are on the side: a power button, an up arrow, and a down arrow. Easy enough.

I turn the toy on and press the up arrow. It buzzes lightly, but it feels like nothing in my palm.

"Press it against the back of your hand," Noelle suggests, and I do as she says, jolting out of my skin as the suction touches me.

"Holy shit."

"Told you," she replies with a grin that turns me on more than the thought of the toy does.

She holds the head of her toy against her clit before turning it on, and a long breath rushes out of her when she does. She looks at me, her skin flushed. "Your turn, sweetheart."

Sweetheart. God. That shouldn't feel so good.

I take a deep breath before spreading my legs and moving the toy down my body. Noelle follows my hand with her eyes, and I swear I feel her gaze like a brand, running over my skin. I press the toy to my clit and immediately slam my free hand against the bed as a shock of pleasure bursts inside me.

"Holy fuck," I cry, pulling the toy away. Jesus, how is that only the first setting? "You were right. That is… Wow."

Noelle lets out a breathy chuckle, nudging my foot playfully with hers. "You can handle it."

I don't entirely believe her, but I suck in a breath and press the toy against my clit again. I'm firmer this time, and the suction feels deeper, less fluttery. It's fucking incredible, though that has as much to do with the sight of Noelle sitting across from me, the feel of her foot brushing against mine, as it does the toy.

"Will you—*fuck*," I groan. It's hard to concentrate with the way the toy feels, radiating heat through my whole body. "Will you tell me what you thought about? What you imagined?"

Noelle bumps the power up on her toy before nodding. "Mhmm. I thought about how you'd taste. Sweet, of course," she says, and I fight to keep my eyes open, to keep them on her. "Lemons. I thought you'd taste like sweet lemons and vanilla. Something bright and summery. You taste"—she raises the power —"so much better," she finishes with a moan.

"I imagined how you'd feel on top of me. I pretended it was your lips instead of the toy. I thought about you between my legs."

I'm still on the lowest speed, but I can't stop the pressure coiling inside me. I'm so fucking close. My eyes close whether I want them to or not, my body slipping back until I'm lying flat on the bed.

"I imagined you looking up at me as you licked my pussy." Noelle's voice sounds simultaneously miles away and like she's whispering right in my ear. I feel the bed shift, but pay no attention until I feel her hand on my calf.

I open my eyes, just in time to watch Noelle straddle my thigh. She rests the toy on my leg and lowers herself onto the head, moaning. Her hair spills around her shoulders like purple silk. She leans down, rolling her hips, riding the toy—riding my thigh. Threading her fingers through my free hand, she presses it against the mattress, holding it down.

She lowers her face, brushing her lips over my jaw, my neck. I feel every little sigh as she gets closer and closer—to me, and to falling apart. All of it, all of her, just amplifies how good the toy feels.

"Guess what, sweetheart?" she murmurs in my ear. Her breath tickles me, and it's almost enough to send me over the edge.

"What?"

"Everything about you is so much better than anything I could ever dream up," she says, pulling my earlobe between her teeth and biting down. It's barely a sting, but it's my undoing.

The orgasm hits me so hard that I drop the toy, and the wave still rolls through me. Noelle follows, crying out my name and letting more of her weight fall on me.

If heaven is real, this must be what it feels like.

I don't realize I'm practically chanting her name until she drags her lips over my jaw and captures my mouth with hers.

"Fuck, Shay," she groans.

She pulls the toy out from under herself and turns it off, tossing it back on the bed. I have no idea where mine is, and, even if Noelle wasn't lying on top of me, I don't think I'd be able to move to turn it off. It's barely audible, and Noelle doesn't seem to care as she shifts her body until she's more cuddled into me than on me.

"Noelle?" I say, clinging to her.

"Hmm?"

"If this is what going with the flow feels like, I think I like it."

Her answering laugh makes my heart stutter.

Oh god. I am so fucked.

21

NOELLE

"*Howshitgonwarinwishay?*"

I stare at my brother, simultaneously disgusted and confused.

"Hell, Felix, maybe try swallowing before talking," my dad chides, pinging him in the ear.

We don't usually do family dinners on Wednesdays, and this one was purely accidental. Shay and I have a day off tomorrow—she's going to visit Nico and is going to be working all weekend to make up for it, so I figured I may as well take the same day off.

Today was draining, but productive. We spent the day prepping and freezing pretty much everything we could, and we're so far ahead of schedule that we could probably take this upcoming weekend off, too, if we wanted to.

I had planned to spend my night lazing around watching TV, but Felix asked if anyone was free to help unpack the first Christmas delivery for The Enchanted Workshop, and I figured I had nothing better to do. Neither, it seemed, did my parents, Rora, or my uncle Henry, who wore Sunny in a baby carrier and almost succeeded in stopping her from putting tinsel in her mouth. Baby girl is already as Christmas-obsessed as the rest of us.

Between the Stanley-Whittens, Abigail, and her brother Quinn, we had everything unpacked and stored away by dinner-time, and my dad promised everyone his famous chili and margaritas as a thank you. No one ever says no to my dad's margaritas.

Felix finishes chewing his cornbread and swallows. "I said, how is it going working with Shay?"

Just the mention of her name has my cheeks heating. "It's going fine," I say, trying to be as vague as possible. "Better than I expected."

"Shay's so nice," Abigail says with a warm smile.

"It's good to see her a bit more involved with the community," my mom chimes in. "And I imagine you both have a lot to learn from each other in the kitchen. What's she like?"

"She's pretty fun, actually. And she's great at what she does. Messy, though. A little loud, but she has good taste in music, at least. She loves ABBA. And she has a cute cat—Croissant."

My mom gasps. "I love ABBA! You know, maybe I should ask her to go for coffee or something. I think we could be good friends."

Yes, because that's exactly what Shay needs: more friends. Granted, she probably could do with a few more friends in town, but I'd really rather my mom wasn't one of them.

"You know, Mom, I'm not sure that would work well, the two of you," I stammer, and my mom pouts.

"How come?"

"Um… Well…"

Rora snorts, and I look over to see her nudging my uncle Henry. "Told you so."

He sighs. "You did, sugar."

However Rora has figured it out, and I'm not surprised because she always does, I would prefer it didn't become a topic of conversation at the dinner table.

My parents are both looking between me and Rora, confused, but everyone else seems clued in.

"It's not that I don't think you and Shay would get along,

Mom, it's just that she's so busy right now with the baking, you know? But I'll mention that you're interested in getting coffee," I say as diplomatically as I can.

This placates my mom, and Rora does me a favor when she immediately changes the subject, asking my parents if they still have a specific photo album from a trip we all took with Rora's parents when we were kids.

My mom ropes my dad into helping her check the attic because she's scared of spiders, and the second they leave, Rora leans forward.

"How long?"

"How long since what?" I ask, feigning ignorance.

"Come on, Noelle, we all know you're sleeping with Shay."

I hold up my hands. "Says who? None of you knows that for sure."

A throat clears, and I turn to look at Quinn, whose cheeks are pink. "Actually, I saw you the other night. You really should consider closing your blinds."

Well, then.

"Thank you, Quinn. Great advice," I say through gritted teeth. "Fine, yes. We've been sleeping together since last week, but it's just sex. Nothing else." There are skeptical faces all around the table, so I continue. "She wants to keep things casual. Apparently, she wants to be friends with me. And anyway, I think she's caught up on the age gap."

I sound… bitter. It's not a good look, but I can't pretend to be happy about it. And I don't want to talk about it. Not here, in front of everyone, anyway.

"It's all good. Things are fine. Hey, at least we're getting along, right?"

I change the subject, asking Quinn and Abigail about their parents instead. Their dad is sick, and a sick parent trumps a situationship conversation-wise.

I sit back and let everyone else talk, fading into the background, thinking about Shay. She didn't seem enthusiastic about visiting Nico tomorrow. I wanted to invite her for dinner, wanted to show her how family can feel. But that's not casual.

As the night wears on, everyone filters out of the kitchen—Felix takes Abigail out back to show her my dad's new garden swing, Quinn sits with my mom and dad to watch the new episode of some crime show they like, Rora and Uncle Henry take Sunny upstairs to change her since she spilled milk all over herself during dinner.

I get started on the dishes. There's something soothing about the repetition of a job like this. I complain about having constant dishes to do at work, but clearing up after a meal my dad made for us, a meal we shared as a family, feels like a privilege.

"Hey. You okay?"

I look over my shoulder to find Rora, my uncle Henry, and Sunny.

"Yeah, I'm fine." I dry my hands on a towel and turn to face them fully.

"We thought you might want this," Uncle Henry says, passing a wriggling Sunny over. "I'll get the dishes."

My niece soothes me immediately; she has the little polar bear blanket she carries everywhere clutched in her hand. I take a seat at the table and hold her close to me, running my hand over the soft peach fuzz covering her head. She grins at me, a toothless smile that feels a lot like staring directly at the sun.

"I needed this. Thank you," I say, smiling as Rora takes a seat opposite me. "I don't know what I'm going to do when she's too big to cuddle like this. You're going to have to give me another one."

She rolls her eyes. "We're working on it."

"What happened to the three of you going traveling when Sunny's six months?" I ask, raising my brows. I'm not surprised they're trying to have another baby, but I am happy it means they'll probably stick around a little longer.

"I don't want Sunny to be an only child. We'll travel once she has a sibling—we don't want to wait too long." She nods toward my uncle Henry and whispers, "Old."

"I heard that, sugar."

Rora shrugs it off. "You were supposed to. I've got to keep you on your toes. Speaking of old… You want to talk about this situation with Shay?"

I snort, surprising a hiccup out of Sunny. "What a segue. Honestly, there's not much to say. I really like her, but that doesn't mean much if she just wants to be friends who sleep together."

"Have you considered, I don't know… communicating a little?" Rora asks, raising a brow.

Communication: a novel concept. It's a nice idea, in theory, but communicating how I feel and what I want means risking Shay telling me she doesn't want the same. And right now, I'm not sure I could handle that. It's stupid and masochistic, but I'm finding it hard to care about that when keeping my mouth shut means I have at least a little part of her.

"Do you think it's your age that's stopping her wanting more?" Rora prods when I say nothing.

I shrug. "I think that's part of it. And yes, I know I should talk to her about all of this. I will. Eventually."

Shay is more complex than I think I even realize. Between her strained relationship with her brother, her deep-rooted trauma about Georgie, and her spending almost two decades married to someone she wasn't in love with purely for convenience's sake, it's a lot to unpack. And it's a lot to ask her to unpack, considering it's only been a week since I kissed her.

"Well, the age gap part we can maybe help you with," Rora reasons. "Don't get me wrong, we're in a great place," she says, nodding between her and Uncle Henry, "but it's not easy. You have completely different life experiences—you grew up in different eras. Not to mention, you have to plan for a future where you'll be at different stages at times. And you have to think about how it feels from Shay's point of view, too. She probably feels pretty shaken for being attracted to someone so much younger—right?"

She directs the question to my uncle Henry, who sets the last plate in the drying rack and turns around. "Oh yeah, it's a lot to grapple with. It took me a while to believe that Rora could even be interested in me. You might just have to give Shay time and keep showing her that you are. But also, be ready for what happens after. We're lucky. No one in our lives cares about the age gap, but you've seen what happens when we leave Wintermore. How often do people mistake me for Rora's dad? Sunny's grandpa? I imagine the comments would be ten times worse for a woman, considering society's shitty double standards."

"I guess I hadn't thought about what it must be like day to day," I admit. For me, it was stranger that Rora was dating my uncle than Rora dating someone so much older than her. We laugh and joke whenever someone mistakes her for his daughter—they look nothing alike—but I hadn't considered the toll that might take.

"Don't get us wrong; we wouldn't change a thing about this," Rora says as he leans down and kisses the top of her head, "but we came into this knowing we had a solid family foundation, and we were both ready for a big change in our lives. I don't know a lot about Shay, but I know she and Nico aren't close, and I know she doesn't have a lot of people here. I'm guessing there's some baggage there."

"Oh yeah. There's a lot of baggage," I confirm. It feels wrong to tell them about any of the things Shay and I have spoken about. They're not secrets—Georgie, her ex-husband, those things are public record, but I get the feeling Shay's not usually as open about them as she has been with me.

"So, what, I just take it slow, hint to her that I want more, and hope she picks up on it?"

"That's what I'd do. For now, anyway," my uncle Henry says. "Y'all are going to be spending a whole hell of a lot of time together over the next few weeks. Use it. Get to know each other better and slowly build on things."

"Patience isn't my strongest attribute," I admit. It's an understatement, and they both know it, but neither of them calls me on it, and I appreciate that. "But I can try. Shay is worth trying for."

"And other than Shay, you're doing alright?" Rora asks, her gaze scrutinizing.

"Of course. Why wouldn't I be?"

"You just haven't seemed… happy, since you opened the bakery," she says, seeing through me as always.

"I'm just tired. It's a lot of work."

"I know, and you're killing it," Rora says, reaching across the table to squeeze my hand. "I'm just saying, it's okay if the thing you've always dreamed about isn't all you thought it would be."

"It's fine. I'm fine," I lie, knowing she won't buy it. If my uncle Henry weren't here, she'd probably push me further, but she just hums.

"Well, you've been happier this week. I assume that's the orgasms."

"Jesus Christ," Uncle Henry says, shaking his head and pushing back from the table while Rora snorts, and I cover Sunny's tiny ears.

22
SHAY

When I wake up on the anniversary of my sister's death, the sky is crying. Thick raindrops pound against the windows, and I curse Mother Nature for making my life just a little more difficult on the day of the year that's already the hardest.

I force myself through the motions of being a human: brushing my teeth, washing my face, pulling on crumpled jeans from the "they're clean enough" pile in my closet. It takes all of ten steps to get from my front door to my car, but I'm soaked through by the time I'm safely inside my little Toyota Camry.

Driving up the mountain isn't my favorite thing to do in the best of conditions, and this visibility is far from the best. Why the fuck did my brother have to move up here? Surely he could have hidden from the world at a more reasonable altitude.

The drive could take ten minutes or ten hours for all I know; I all but black out every time I have to drive up here.

Nico is waiting for me when I finally pull up outside his cabin, sitting on his covered porch with two giant piles of fluff that are more like wolves than dogs, and two thermoses. I didn't tell him I was coming, but I didn't have to. Not because of the weird triplet connection we have, but because I show up every year.

This day holds a lot of good memories, but every one of them died the second Georgie's heart stopped.

I steel myself before climbing out of the car.

"Happy birthday," I call, turning away to close my door so we don't have to look at each other when we say it.

"Happy birthday, Shay."

We're both quiet for a second, leaving space for a third birthday greeting that we still can't bring ourselves to say, all these years later.

Georgie was the best of us: the brightest, the prettiest, the smartest, the most liked. I don't say it to be self-deprecating—it's a fact. She grew into herself a little earlier than Nico and I did. It's like she woke up at sixteen and had it all figured out, while we were still in the awkward teenage phase of our lives.

I've heard that some triplets and twins resent each other when they grow at different paces, but we never did. We looked at Georgie with pride, and we knew we had plenty of time to figure our shit out. Maybe, deep down, Georgie knew she didn't have as much time as we did. Or maybe the world is just fundamentally unfair. I guess we'll never know for sure.

"How was the drive?" Nico asks as I hurry up the porch steps and take a seat across from him. The dogs lift their heads, glaring at me in unison. Like my brother, they're not much for people. They barely tolerate me, but they love him.

Nico hands me a thermos, and I take a long drag of warm coffee before answering.

"Shit. It's always shit."

"You need a better car."

I raise a brow at him. "You need a better address."

"Better than this?" Nico gestures to the surrounding trees. Mountains tower over the horizon, and there's a bird of prey calling somewhere in the distance. He has a point.

"How have you been?" I ask, changing the subject, because his choice to live up here is a dead horse at this point.

Nico shrugs, and I can see him clam up a little. "You know. Same old, same old." His voice is scratchy, like it's been a while since he spoke out loud. It probably has been. Our conversations are mostly texts, and he has exactly one friend, whom I know he barely talks to. He occasionally drives down the mountain for work or to stock up on supplies in Jackson, and he calls our parents every couple of weeks, but he's not exactly chatty.

"How are things with you?" he asks.

"Pretty much the same. The movie's going well. I think it is, anyway. We don't have a lot to do with it beyond handing over whatever they've asked us to make, but everyone seems happy. And the town's super busy, so that's been good, customer-wise. Actually, I got an order last week for a birthday cake…" I continue to talk about everything and nothing, and Nico nods and grunts, absentmindedly stroking the dogs, and playing at paying attention. It's the same song and dance every time I come here.

It's not that he doesn't care what I have to say; it's just that whatever I'm talking about isn't his main focus. He'd never admit it, but I know it's hard for Nico to look at me and see anything but Georgie. We weren't identical, but we were close. Her hair was a little lighter, her eyes a little darker, her nose a little sharper. She was objectively prettier, but that had everything to do with how she presented herself. It's hard to imagine how she would be now, but I like to think we'd still look as alike at forty-seven as we did at twenty-five.

Forty-seven. God.

My parents struggle to look at me, too. It's one of the reasons I finally gave up on California and moved out here.

Nico moved to Wintermore a year after Georgie died. She had two obsessions: France and cheesy holiday movies. When *A*

Christmas Wish in the Mountains released, she watched it on repeat for months. We were going to surprise her with a trip to Wintermore as a birthday gift, but we were on our way to our birthday dinner when the accident happened.

Georgie never did find out about the plane tickets tucked inside her birthday card.

I liked Wintermore the first time I flew out to visit Nico, but I didn't make the move until my divorce. When the payment came through from my half of the house, at the same time as the café on Main Street went on the market, it seemed like fate. Georgie and I always talked about opening a patisserie when we lived in Paris, and suddenly I could make her dream come true in her favorite town. How could I not make it happen?

I naively thought it would bring Nico and me closer in more than proximity, but our relationship remains largely "how have you been?" and "anything new for you?" It's like we're scared to open up about anything of substance in case it brings up ghosts from the past. Everything always comes back to Georgie.

And every time I do try to talk, he shuts me down. There used to be nothing we didn't talk about, and I miss it. I miss having someone to talk to, and Nico has, too. It can't be good for either of us to keep things so surface-level.

I finish my coffee and clear my throat. "You know how I was kind of into women before Philippe and I got married?"

Nico's expression doesn't change, but there's a flash of confusion in his eyes—gray, but darker than mine and Georgie's. "Kind of into women?" he asks slowly. "What the hell are you talking about 'kind of'? Shay, you exclusively dated women from the ages of sixteen to twenty-five."

"Right. But it's been a while, obviously. I haven't thought about who I'm interested in since I was married for so long, and it's not like I've dated since the divorce."

Surprise lights Nico's face. "At all?"

I shake my head, drumming my nails on the thermos. "I tried. I downloaded the apps, even spoke to a couple of people, but no one clicked."

"And I assume, since you're talking about it now, that you've met someone?"

"Kind of. Yeah." I sigh, and Nico gestures for me to go on. "It's complicated."

"Because she's a woman? You can't seriously still be worried about upsetting Mom and Dad. I think enough time has passed since…" Nico trails off, shadows gathering in his eyes.

"It's not that," I hurry to say.

"Is she married?"

"No. She's… thirty."

Nico's so stoic that even I can't always discern what the micro-changes in his expression mean, but the eyebrow he raises is pretty damn clear. At least it distracts him from almost talking about Georgie. "Well, shit. I mean, thirty is young, but I guess it's not *that* young. Just feels like a lifetime ago."

"That it does," I say dryly.

"Hey, no judgment," Nico says, holding his hands up. "Personally, I could never be with someone seventeen years younger than me, but if you're into her, and she's into you—wait, *is* she into you?"

"It's just over sixteen years," I correct, because it makes *so* much difference. "That's also complicated." I groan, rubbing my face. "I'm pretty sure she's into me. She used to hate me, but we've been spending a lot of time together, and she's warmed up to me. I told her I wanted to be friends, and she didn't balk."

"Why the hell did you tell her you wanted to be friends if you want more than that?"

That is the million-dollar question. "She mentioned a few weeks ago that she's too busy to date and she was just looking for something casual," I grumble. *Casual.* That word is fucking haunting me. I keep saying it, trying to drill it into my brain, hoping I might actually start believing that's what I want, too, eventually.

"She mentioned it in passing, or she specifically said that's what she wanted with you?" Nico asks.

Technically, she mentioned it when she still hated me, but that's not the point. In the three weeks since our first meeting with Mayor Blackwood, I've witnessed Noelle working her ass off, day in and day out. I see how much people ask of her, but moreover, I see how much she asks of herself. I'm not going to be another person asking her to give more of herself than she's got.

"In passing, then," Nico surmises from my silence. "Shay. Just talk to the woman."

"It's—"

"If you say complicated again, I'm going to be pissed," Nico interrupts, and I close my mouth, because that's exactly what I was going to say.

I'm old enough to know how to communicate like a goddamn adult. But there's something about Noelle that just… scares the shit out of me. I know I need to talk to her, but I'm terrified to tell her I want more and potentially lose what we do have. For the first time in a long time, I don't feel so lonely.

"Look, are you interested in her? Like really interested?"

"I think so?" He looks unimpressed by my answering a question with a question. "I don't know. I mean, yes, I am, but I feel like I have no idea what I'm doing, and Noelle just seems to have everything figured out."

Nico narrows his eyes. "Noelle Whitten? That's who you're talking about?"

"Yeah. Have you met her?"

"Briefly," he answers with a shrug. "You know her sister owns the other cabin up here?"

I nod, not bothering to correct him that Noelle and Rora's relationship is far more complicated than sisters.

"Well, I know Rora fairly well, and I've met her partner. He's around our age, if not older, so I don't think you have to be worried about the age gap scandalizing Noelle or her family."

"I think I'm more bothered about it than she is," I admit.

Nico snorts. "Look, I'm not the best person to offer relationship advice, but what do you have to lose? Like you said, she used to hate you. There's no guarantee you'd be friends after the movie is over anyway."

He's nothing if not blunt, but he's not wrong.

"That's true. But Noelle seems so sure of herself—if she was interested, I'm sure she'd make it known."

I worry my lower lip until Nico sighs. "There's no harm in just having fun with her while you're working together and having a bigger conversation when filming's almost over. And even if Noelle's not interested, it wouldn't hurt to try and meet people. You don't need to look for anything serious, but you deserve to have a little fun, Shay. Seriously, when was the last time you did?"

"When was the last time *you* did anything fun?" I volley back, because it's easier to focus on Nico than myself. "Have you agreed to meet up with Bryan yet?" Bryan has been Nico's best friend since we were all in kindergarten together, and he's the only person who stuck around after Georgie died and Nico shut everyone else out. Not that he hasn't tried to shut Bryan out— Nico hasn't seen him since he moved to Wintermore. He didn't go to Bryan's wedding, or the ceremony where he adopted his new husband's daughters, or any of the important life events Bryan still, to this day, invites our family to.

Bryan was never my best friend, but I think I speak to him more than Nico does, thanks to Facebook. I know he's asked Nico to come visit, and offered to come here, and I know Nico has declined every invitation.

I watch as my question sinks into my brother, watch as his walls shoot right back up. He stands, grabbing both of our coffee cups and heading toward the cabin door. "We're not talking about me. Refill?"

He's inside, shutting me down, before I can even answer.

23
SHAY

If I go too long without visiting Nico, I get antsy. It's a triplet thing, I suppose. Everything feels a little hollow without him. Since Georgie died, I've had a gaping hole that I don't think anyone could ever fill, but spending time with Nico recharges me a little.

And also thoroughly exhausts me.

It's my fault, really. If I treaded shallower waters and stopped bringing things up that I know he won't want to talk about, I probably wouldn't leave feeling like I've spent hours repeatedly hitting my head against a brick wall every time I see him. But I miss the relationship we used to have. I miss having someone I could talk to about anything. I didn't just lose Georgie in the accident.

Nico always offers me a spare room for the night if I want to stay, and I always decline. It's too quiet on the mountain for me to sleep. The drive down isn't nearly as bad as the drive up, but I'm dead on my feet as I drag myself up the stairs to my apartment. At least the rain has cleared up, though that hasn't stopped Croissant from spending a whole day snoozing on his favorite blanket on my couch, it seems. I get changed into my comfiest sleep tee, kiss his head, and join him with my own favorite blanket, because I know he doesn't like to share.

I flick through the TV, but nothing catches my attention. The age of streaming has made it impossible to mindlessly watch TV. There are too many choices, and I get overwhelmed trying to choose. When I lived with Philippe, he always picked what we watched because I could never decide.

I miss having someone to talk to on quiet nights like this, but it's not Philippe's company I'm craving. Before I can overthink it, my phone is in my hand.

> Hey. Are you awake?

It's after ten, but three dots immediately pop up on my screen, and Noelle's reply follows a second later:

> Did you really just send me a "you up?" text?

> I sent you a text to ask if you're awake, if that's what that is.

> It's not.

> A "you up?" text usually implies a booty call.

> Huh. I'm rethinking my reason for texting you now.

> If this isn't a booty call (☹) then what's up?

It's amazing how much just talking to her lifts my mood. I'm still sitting alone in my apartment (not counting Croissant, who's snoring and paying no attention to me), but I don't feel so alone.

> I was wondering if you had any TV show recommendations.

It sounds stupid the second I send it, and the message stays unanswered for long enough that I think Noelle is just going to ignore it. In reality, it's only a minute, but it feels like an hour until my screen finally changes. Not with a text, but a call.

"That's a loaded question," Noelle says the second I answer, forgoing a greeting, "I have a lot of recommendations. How long do you have?"

Her voice does something funny and twisty to my insides.

"However long it takes," I answer, and she laughs.

"Perfect. What kinds of things do you usually watch?"

I explain that I don't watch a lot of TV, but rhyme off a few of the shows I liked watching with Philippe, and she hums.

"Have you started your annual fall *Gilmore Girls* rewatch yet?"

"My… what?" I've never heard that collection of words together in my life.

"You know, your yearly *Gilmore Girls* marathon?"

"I've never seen it," I say, and you would think I'd confessed to murder for the scream she lets out.

"That has to change immediately. I'm coming over. Be there in ten."

She hangs up, leaving me gaping at my phone. That was… so Noelle.

I glance around the apartment, making sure nothing looks too messy. It's not like she hasn't seen me surrounded by mess, but my apartment is generally tidier than my workspace. And it is tonight, thankfully. I consider changing, because a decade-old Dollywood T-shirt isn't what I'd usually wear to receive guests, but I don't have nice PJs, and I don't want to look like I'm trying too hard.

There's no time to change, anyway, because Noelle knocks on my door in exactly seven minutes, not ten.

I open the door, and she holds up two cups. "I brought coffee."

Ignoring the way my heart flutters at the sight of her, I take the offered cup. "It's after ten. Is coffee a good idea?"

"It's decaf, and trust me, it's impossible to watch *Gilmore Girls* and not want coffee," she says with a shrug before leaning in and pressing a kiss so fast and light to my lips, it's over before I realize what's happening. "Hi."

"Hi," I repeat, and she grins at me, closing my front door behind her and making her way to my couch.

"How did you make it to forty-six without seeing *Gilmore Girls*?" she asks, scratching Croissant behind the ears and sitting beside him. He graces her with one single cracked eye before going back to sleep.

"Forty-seven," I say, sounding only a little bitter about my new age. "And like I said on the phone, I pretty much watched whatever Philippe wanted."

I sit beside her, and she turns to me, frowning.

"Forty-seven? Since when?"

Shit. "Um. Since midnight?"

Noelle's eyes widen. "Midnight… like today?" I nod, and she immediately whacks me in the arm. "What the hell? Why didn't you tell me it was your birthday?"

I chuckle, capturing the hand that whacked me with mine, twining our fingers together. "I'm not a big birthday person."

"Hmm. Well, happy birthday, sweetheart," she says, her expression softening. She puts her coffee cup down on the table and leans in to kiss me. This one is longer, slower, and quite possibly the best birthday present I've ever had. She tastes rich like coffee, and decaf or not, she wakes me up.

"Is that why you went to visit Nico today? For your birthday?"

I nod, wondering how much to tell her, how much to open up. Noelle has met every vulnerability I've given her with empathy and understanding, and I feel like I'd be doing her a disservice if I didn't trust her with this one.

"Today's not just our birthday. It's the anniversary of the accident."

Sympathy floods her eyes, her hand tightening around mine. "Oh my god, Shay. I'm so sorry. How are you holding up?"

I lift one shoulder in a shrug. "It's been twenty-two years, and in some ways, it feels like it was yesterday. But in others, it's like it was a lifetime ago. It was, I suppose."

I toy with my locket, and Noelle reaches out, tracing the G with her pinky.

"What do you think she would have been like at forty-seven?" she asks, once again surprising me with her willingness, *eagerness* to talk about something most people shy away from.

Something *I've* shied away from for too long.

"Georgie was the kind of person who, when she wanted something, she made it happen. She always wanted to be a mom, so I guess she'd have a few kids running around, and she wanted a horse, even though she knew nothing about horses." I smile at the memory of Georgie flicking through the equestrian catalog she found god knows where, talking about all the things she'd buy for her hypothetical horse. "We would probably still have the patisserie, I guess. I don't know what it would look like, but I bet it would've been here. She would've loved it here so much she wouldn't have wanted to leave."

"I wish I'd gotten to meet her," Noelle says softly, cuddling into my side. "She sounds special, and if she was anything like you, I know I'd l—I think we'd get along."

"She would have loved you," I say without thinking. But she would have. If she were here, Georgie would have befriended the whole town, but especially the Whittens. Especially Noelle. She loved Christmas and cozy things, and they would've gotten along like a house on fire.

And if she knew I was interested, she would have told me to get over myself and do something about it. She would've told me to take the word "casual" out of my vocabulary and tell Noelle how I feel. And that thought makes me a little more brave. Not brave enough to tell her I don't want to be friends, but brave enough to wrap my arm around her shoulders, pull her in closer to me, and press a kiss to her forehead.

Noelle sighs, a soft, happy sound.

"I'm glad you're here," I say quietly.

"Me too. Thank you for sharing your birthday with me, even if I did just barge in here," she replies with a laugh.

"You had a noble cause." I grab my TV remote and pull up *Gilmore Girls*, hovering over the first episode. "*Gilmore Girls*?"

"Oh yeah," Noelle says, taking the remote from my hand and pulling up the first episode. "I'm about to change your life, sweetheart."

Oh boy, she has no idea.

24

NOELLE

I'm not good at taking time off, but I still feel guilty that I didn't find out about Shay's birthday until the day was almost over, so when she suggests taking the following Sunday off to spend the day together, I jump at the chance. We're quickly approaching the end of our time working together, and I want to cling to every moment I can get with her.

A few days ago, pillow-talking breathlessly, I asked Shay where her favorite place in Wintermore was, and she didn't even have to think before answering. "The reservoir. I love it there. Georgie loved water, and I can see the mountains, so I always feel closer to her and Nico there. I've considered renting a boat a few times to go out on the water, but I've never rowed a boat before," she said, and I started planning straight away.

I don't have a boat, but my parents do. It's nothing fancy, just a little wooden rowboat that we used to take out on the reservoir when we were kids. My parents still go out for boat picnics every summer, and the storm from earlier this week has left behind an unseasonably warm fall weekend. The perfect weather for a picnic, if you ask me.

When I called to ask if I could borrow the boat, my dad didn't ask questions. As I park my car outside their house, I realize I'm not going to get away so easily: my mom is helping my dad secure the boat on the bed of their truck, a wicker basket at her feet. I should've known.

"Hi, honey!" she calls as I get out of my car.

"Hey."

I grab *my* picnic basket (tote bag) from the trunk, even though I know it won't be half as impressive as whatever my mom has put together. When you treat every day like Christmas, every day is a cause for celebration, and every celebration deserves a feast— that's my mom's outlook, anyway. And no one in their right mind would ever turn down any kind of food packed by either of my parents. I fell in love with the kitchen, standing on a little wooden step stool so I could reach the counters and bake with them, but my food will never taste as good as theirs. They put so much love into everything they do.

"Thank you for getting the boat out for me and letting me use the truck," I say, hugging my dad, then my mom.

"Anytime, kiddo."

"What's the occasion?" My mom leans against the truck, the fall sunshine catching the threads of gold in her auburn hair.

"Does there need to be an occasion? It's a beautiful day," I counter, and she snorts.

"Don't bullshit us. You never do this kind of thing, and your dad isn't nearly nosy enough." She prods him in the side, and he yelps. "Who, pray tell, are you taking on a romantic boat trip on this beautiful day?"

"You called it romantic, not me," I point out, but there's no point in dodging around it. Quinn already spotted Shay and me together; it's only a matter of time before someone else does, and this town is a breeding ground for gossip.

"Shay and I are… seeing each other, I guess."

"You guess? What does that mean?" my dad asks, frowning at me.

"It means it's complicated," I answer, because I really don't want to explain the ins and outs of whatever the hell is going on between us. Mostly because I can't. We're sleeping together… casually. We snuggled on her couch and watched *Gilmore Girls* until we both fell asleep a couple of days ago… casually. I'm taking her on a romantic boat trip today… casually.

"But you're interested in her?" my mom asks, looking completely unsurprised. I assume the rumor mill is already turning.

"I am. We're just figuring things out."

"Well, we're happy for you either way, kiddo," my dad says, squeezing my shoulder. "I know she's a bit older than you, but hey, at least she's not family-adjacent."

I snort. "I suppose it would be hard to scandalize you after Rora and Uncle Henry."

"Don't say that around Felix," my mom warns with a shudder. "I hate to think how he would take that as a challenge."

She talks me through everything she packed in the picnic basket—half the contents of her kitchen, it seems—until I eventually drag myself away, tossing them my car keys in case they need the car, and climbing into their truck with a wave.

Shay is standing outside when I pull up. I didn't tell her the plan for today, just to dress to be outside, and her eyes widen as she takes in my parents' truck with the rowboat strapped to the bed.

Croissant winds around her feet, meowing as I jump down from the truck and round the cab.

"Hi, baby," I coo, crouching down and gathering him into my arms. I stand up, stepping closer to his mom.

"You know, when you said you had a surprise for me, I was expecting you to show up with The Grinch butt plug," she says, surprising a laugh from me.

"Even I don't love Christmas enough to use The Grinch butt plug." I lean in to kiss her. "Hi, sweetheart."

"Hi. That's a boat."

"Sure is. What do you reckon?" I ask Croissant, scratching his chin. "You want to come with your mama and I for a picnic on the reservoir?" He meows, and I take that as a yes.

"We're going to the reservoir?" Shay asks, practically vibrating with excitement.

"If you want to," I answer, but I barely get the words out before she says, "Yes!"

I open the passenger door and deposit Croissant on the seat. The reservoir isn't big, and we'll never be so far out that we won't be able to drop him off at the shore if he doesn't like the boat, but I have a blanket, and no doubt he'll happily snuggle in and watch the birds go by.

Shay climbs up beside him while I get back behind the wheel, and her smile is brighter than the blazing fall sunshine.

It's a short drive to the reservoir; usually, I'd walk, but despite years of hauling palettes of toys and sacks of flour, I don't think I could carry the boat the whole way.

And the short drive is more than worth it when Shay sighs happily and says, "How is it possible that you look this hot driving?" She squeezes my knee, and I practically melt.

Shay helps me unload the boat, and I get the food and blankets situated while she carries Croissant. Once the two of them are settled, I lock the truck and push the boat over the last of the rocky shore. I hop in right before the current pulls the boat, feeling the ground disappear beneath me as the weightlessness of the water takes over.

The view of the mountains, of the sun glistening on the water's surface, is incredible. But I can't stop looking at Shay.

She stares around us in wonder, taking in every inch of the scene. There's a soft breeze, enough to cool the heat of the sun and tease the ends of her hair. Even Croissant looks enraptured, scrunching his little nose and looking around wide-eyed.

"You know," Shay whispers, like she's scared to speak too loudly and disturb the peace, "I've been a lot of places in my life, but I think this might be my favorite."

"It's pretty magical," I agree. "I should bring you here at night sometime. The stars are incredible."

"I can imagine."

She sets Croissant down like a loaf on one of the blankets I brought and steps gingerly over the center seat so she can sit facing me. Our knees brush, the tiny touch enough to make my heart race.

"Thank you for doing this. It's even better than I dreamed it would be." She cups my cheek, and my skin warms beneath her touch.

I bring her hand to my mouth, pressing my lips to her palm. "I'm glad I got to be the one to share it with you." The words spill out, anything but casual, but I can't bring myself to regret a little scrap of honesty somewhere so beautiful.

"Did I hear you say picnic?"

"Mhmm." I lift the picnic basket and balance it on the bench seat beside me. "I made sandwiches and packed some treats, but when I picked up the boat, my mom had the basket with practically an entire grocery store in it for us, so we're stocked."

She doesn't respond as I unzip the basket, and when I look up, she's frowning. "What?"

"You told your parents about us?"

Ah. Shit. She doesn't sound pissed, just confused, at least.

"Yes, but in my defense, they definitely already knew," I answer quickly.

She looks no less confused. If anything, her eyebrows climb higher.

Croissant chooses this moment to perk up, crawling under the bench his mom is sitting on, and standing up on his hind legs to investigate the food.

I toss him a snap pea, and he chases it around the floor.

"Are people talking about us?" Shay asks, and I can't ascertain how she feels about the possibility from her measured tone.

"This is Wintermore," I answer with a shrug. "I think it's safe to assume someone is talking about you at all times. But us? I don't know. My parents weren't surprised when I told them who was coming with me today, and I know my brother's friend, Quinn, spotted us through my window a few days ago, so I'm guessing other people in town have also noticed."

"Shit." Shay worries her bottom lip with her teeth. "I suppose we haven't been as careful as we should've been."

I have to force myself not to show how much I don't like that.

"Are you upset that people know?"

Every second that Shay takes to think about her answer feels longer.

It's not fair of me, I know. She doesn't know this town like I do; she doesn't know my family like I do. Shay has every right to feel whatever kind of way she feels about people knowing we're… doing something, even if I'm not sure either of us knows what said something is.

"I'm not upset," she says, finally. "You're right that we should probably have assumed people would talk. I just don't like the idea of being spoken about behind my back—and I like the idea of you being spoken about even less."

Oh. As far as answers go, that could've been a lot worse. I was ready for it to hurt.

"I know it doesn't make it better or easier, but I'm used to it. I was born in a small town in Texas, and I've lived in Wintermore for over twenty years. It comes with the territory."

"I guess that's true. How were your parents about it?"

"They were fine with it," I assure her, and relief flickers in her gray eyes. "Just like I said they would be. To quote my dad, 'at least you're not family-adjacent.'"

Her laugh is so fucking pretty. She throws her head back, and the sun catches her hair, lighting her up like a sparkling fire. It's hard to believe how long I spent in denial about how beautiful she is. How funny she is, how smart she is, how sweet, and soft, and perfect she is. How desperately I want her. Maybe even need her.

It's funny, really. This time two years ago, all I wanted was to open my bakery and watch the downfall of Shay's. Now, I can't help but think I'd like to stay out here forever and forget my bakery even exists.

25
NOELLE

It's funny how time flies when the future is full of unknowns. I thought my time working with Shay would drag, that I would be counting down the days until we were finished. But now, we're a week from the movie wrapping, and our work is dwindling.

Every day, I've been coming down to the basement kitchen a little earlier, leaving a little later, usually with Shay's hand in mine. The Enchanted Bakery isn't suffering as much as I thought it would be in my absence; my staff have stepped up. Maybe I got so used to working with Felix that I didn't give them enough credit. Maybe I'm not as needed as I thought I was. And maybe I'm okay with that.

No, I'm definitely okay with that. Even if it's just for now, so I can savor the last week of working with Shay, I'm grateful not to be needed. The Enchanted Bakery is closed for a whole week while the crew films whatever they need, and I can put all of my focus on baking for the movie. Baking with Shay.

I like baking with her, and I hate baking upstairs. There's something to unpack there, I'm just not quite sure how to go about it. But I know I need to figure it out, and soon, because this time next week we'll be hanging up our aprons and going our separate ways—albeit, we'll still be across the street from each other, but we won't be baking together. I don't know if we'll be doing anything together.

We never put a deadline on whatever this is, but we also haven't spoken about the ins and outs of it since we agreed to keep sleeping together. It's easy not to talk about it when we're always around each other, when we don't have to try and make plans if we want to spend time together. It's just an assumption at this point that we'll be hanging out after work every night. I don't remember the last time we didn't, and I'm struggling to imagine what "after" looks like.

I don't want to stop seeing her. I don't want to give this up. I don't want to be her friend, and I don't want this to be "casual." But I know what my life looks like when I'm not working on the movie, and I know how little time I have for anything outside of work. Sure, my staff is holding down the fort now, but tourist season is just beginning. I can't ask them to add more and more to their plates, and I've hired everyone in town with any kind of experience. I don't have time to train someone from scratch right as the busy season starts.

Shay would understand if I explained that I have to check out for a few months until after Christmas. I know she would—god knows she'll be busier, too. But I don't want to check out. I don't want my life to go back to how it was two months ago. I've gotten used to enjoying my life a little more.

I look up, watching Shay laminating dough of some kind, silently mouthing the words to a French song I don't recognize. It's been just over a month since Sunny swiped yes on her Locked profile. Just over a month of doing everything I can to memorize the lines on her face, the soft cadence of her voice, the warm, cozy aura she emanates. I've gotten used to being a part of Shay's life and having her in mine. And I don't want to give it up.

As if she can feel my gaze, Shay glances up, her lips curving into a smile when she sees I'm watching her.

"You look like you're thinking pretty hard over there, *mon délice*."

"I can't just admire you working?"

She narrows her eyes, but there's no heat in them. "Hmm. What are you thinking about?"

"Just thinking about how fast the past month has gone. The movie's almost finished," I answer honestly. "I guess I'm wondering what life will look like after, you know?"

Storm clouds roll through Shay's eyes, and she looks away, turning her attention back to the dough. She might as well have physically slammed a door in my face.

"It'll be nice to get a parking space at the grocery store again," she says after what feels like an age. There's a forced levity to her voice, and I'm not going to push, even if I want to.

"That's true. At least until the Christmas tourists arrive." I busy my hands, dumping a bowl of hazelnuts on my chopping board and running my knife through them. A food processor would be more efficient, but not nearly as satisfying.

"Thai food tonight? I'm feeling something spicy," Shay says, like she's trying to get us back on even footing.

"Whatever you want, sweetheart," I answer. It's not hard to smile at her, but it's hard to make it reach my eyes all the way. "*Gilmore Girls*?"

"Of course."

We're already almost finished season five, which is a testament to just how much time we've been spending together. Sometimes we watch while we're working, but mostly we snuggle up in one of our beds with Croissant. Shay is Team Logan, and I suppose everyone needs to have a flaw.

I love curling up with her, but these days, all I can think about is whether we'll get the chance to finish the series when we're no longer working together. It's entirely possible she's going to call this whole thing off in a week, and, if so, our last few days will be tainted by uncertainty and anxiety.

How will she spend Christmas? How does she usually spend Christmas? I can't imagine Nico is much in the way of company. How will she spend her paycheck from the movie? She mentioned wanting to do some work on *Épices et Sucré* weeks ago, but never specifics. I want to be there—to help, if I can. I want to spend Christmas with her and take her to the reservoir on New Year's Eve to watch the fireworks.

I want more. I need more.

I need Shay.

But right now, it feels as much of a fantasy as the taste of her did all those weeks ago. And this time, I have no idea how to turn this fantasy into reality.

26

SHAY

My body all but collapses onto the bed at the plastic click of the harness clasp. The sound sends a zing of anticipation through me every time I hear it, and I'm already on edge and sensitive from the three orgasms she's given me tonight.

Something feels… different. Noelle has seemed off all day, and I'm in denial about what that means. She tried to talk about it earlier, and I shut her down, because we have less than a week of working together left, and I'm not ready to think about what comes next.

There are three outcomes I can see, each one getting less likely. The first—and most likely—scenario in my head is that filming wraps, Noelle goes back to being run off her feet at work, and gently breaks that she doesn't have time for us to keep hanging out. I don't think she'll go back to hating me—I hope not, anyway. If she does, I might just have to move in with Nico and never show my face around here again.

I find it hard to see an outcome where this friendship or whatever we're calling it is maintainable as it is, but that's still more likely than the third scenario: she wants more than casually hanging out and hooking up. The idea that she would want that, with me of all people, is laughable.

But things have felt less casual lately. The boat trip, telling her parents about us, the late nights and early mornings, the way she just watches me sometimes… It's fucking with my head, telling me there's a tiny, minute chance she wants this like I do.

And I don't think I can risk the heartbreak of asking her and being let down. That's why I changed the subject earlier, when I could tell she wanted to talk about what comes next. Denial is as safe as it gets right now.

And denial doesn't feel half bad when it involves Noelle's fingers digging into my hips as she pushes the smooth dildo into me with a curse.

"Oh, fuck," she groans, her fingers pressing almost painfully into my skin. It feels incredible.

Noelle's toy collection is bordering on hoarding, but no complaints from me. I've enjoyed everything we've tried, though that probably has more to do with who I'm trying them with than the toys themselves. Her collection puts the fifteen-year-old rabbit I found at the back of a dingy lingerie store at the mall to shame. I've been missing out.

This particular one seems to be a favorite of hers, though. The harness itself is much simpler than the ones she has on her wall— a mix of pleather, elastic, plastic clasps, and a few decorative chain links—but she favors it over the fancier ones, and she makes my mouth water every time I watch her put it on.

It has two pink vibrating dildos, one for each of us, and Noelle explained that every movement *I* feel, she feels. And it feels fucking incredible. Every brush of the silicone inside me is like Noelle is striking a match, over and over again, until we're consumed by flames.

She leans over me, covering my body with hers, pressing a kiss to the back of my head as she fucks me. I push up on my arms with difficulty, and she runs her hand down my torso. She brushes her thumb over my nipple, gently at first, then not at all. She pinches, and I cry out, clenching her flannel sheets.

Christmas sheets, of course. I've gotten so used to falling apart in Noelle's collection of Christmas bedding that I'm worried I'm going to have a Pavlovian response to the extra Christmas decor that pops up in Wintermore come November.

Noelle pulls me up to my knees, my back pressed against her front, her hand clasped gently around my throat. She's not squeezing or restricting my airway in any way, but the fact that she could… Fuck. My head falls back against her shoulder, and I clench around the dildo, my legs shaking.

She thrusts into me as her fingers find my clit, and my vision goes black for a split second.

"Oh god," I moan, pressing my body back into her.

"You better not be giving god credit for how good I'm making you feel, sweetheart," Noelle whispers in my ear, her breath tickling me.

She lifts the hand around my throat so it's cupping my chin and turns my head so she can press a kiss against my burning cheek. She drags her lips down, over my jaw, and into the curve of my shoulder, nipping my skin with her teeth, then blowing cool air over the spot.

The quick rush of sensation tips me over the edge, and I tumble into a blissful feeling of everything and nothing all at once. My body lights up, and I can feel Noelle everywhere, from the tips of my toes to the top of my head to the marrow in my bones.

I'm vaguely aware of Noelle crying my name, her arms looping around my body and tightening as she falls apart. We both slip forward, falling against the mattress, a trembling, breathless mess, but the new position only presses the dildo harder against my G-spot, and another wave of pleasure rocks through me.

I'm weightless, floating outside of my own body, my mind empty of everything but Noelle. She pulls out of me, and I cry in protest, but it dies on my lips when, a moment later, her tongue is all over my pussy.

"You. Taste. Fucking. Incredible. Sweetheart." She punctuates each word with a lick before rubbing her tongue over my clit. I'm so sensitive that I'm gone with the first touch, pulling the bedsheets so hard that I feel the corner pop off the mattress, as Noelle draws the fifth? Sixth? Orgasm of the night out of me. I've lost track at this point.

My body is liquid, a pliant puddle. Noelle moves around with ease as she lies down beside me and nudges me until we're both on our sides, nose to nose.

"Holy shit," I pant. "I don't think I've exerted my body this much since high school."

My vision is hazy, but I'm pretty sure she raises her brows. "Damn. We had very different high school experiences."

"I did triathlon," I say, halfheartedly tugging the ends of her hair.

"My previous comment still stands. Head elf of the Christmas Club, remember? I wasn't exactly an athlete."

I laugh, but I'm still so out of breath that it comes out more like a wheeze. "I imagine in a town like this, head elf is a role more coveted than quarterback."

"Oh, yeah. I was a big deal around here."

"You still are," I point out, and she wrinkles her nose. "I can't imagine you in high school," I continue, changing the subject, because I know how uncomfortable the weight of Wintermore's expectations makes her. "Don't get me wrong, I can absolutely imagine you as head elf, but I can imagine you doing that now, too. I know you're a lot younger than me, but I guess it just feels like you have everything figured out. Like you've always had everything figured out. You're so sure of yourself."

"I'm pretty sure of myself, that's true," Noelle agrees. She cups the side of my face, absentmindedly drawing her finger over my cheek in a way that makes me think she's playing connect-the-freckle. "But I don't have everything figured out. Honestly? I feel like I have exactly nothing figured out right now." Her finger stills on the freckle beside my mouth. "Can I tell you a secret?"

"Anything," I murmur, and I think my heart might beat all the way through my ribcage and out of my chest, because I don't think I can handle her telling me she doesn't want to do this anymore right now.

"I think…" She hesitates, biting her lip and scrunching up her face. It's adorable. "I think I kind of hate owning the bakery."

That is… not what I expected her to say.

"Shit," I respond, because I'm not sure what else to say. "What do you hate about it?"

"Everything?" she replies, rolling onto her back and staring up at the ceiling. I mirror her, taking in the twinkling glow-in-the-dark stars. When I asked about them, she said she and Rora had them in their rooms as kids, and she wanted to keep them with her when she moved out because they remind her of Rora.

"Okay, maybe not everything," she amends, "but I feel like I'm being stretched in a million different directions every day, and I never get to just bake. When I do bake, I'm rushing so much that I don't enjoy it, and the baking is what I wanted to do, you know? And I know admin is just part of owning a business, I get it, but that's not really the problem. I spend most of my time out front because people get disappointed if they come in and I'm not there. I understand how lucky I am, and that the town has been nothing but good to me, but god… Do you ever wish you could just bake and not worry about all the other stuff?"

Her eyes are dull, like tumbled sapphires, and I want nothing more than to put the sparkle back where it belongs. I scoot closer to her, lifting my arm over her and running my hand down her back. Her eyes flutter closed.

"I've worked in a lot of kitchens over the years. Honestly, I thought the biggest perk of owning my own place in a small town would be getting to spend more time engaging with people and immersing myself in the community. But it's been lonelier than I expected. I've spent so long keeping to myself, scared to put myself out there, that now I pretty much never leave the kitchen."

I worry that Noelle will think it's stupid. After all, her problems are out of her hands, and mine have been because I've been holding myself back, but when she opens her eyes, she just looks concerned for me.

"I know it's easier said than done, but you should let people in. The people here really like you, sweetheart. Trust me, more people than I can count have spent the past few years trying to convince me you're nice. They were right, obviously, but don't tell anyone I said that," she warns, scowling so dramatically that I can't help but laugh.

"Noted. But you're also right, if it helps. I know I need to let people in more." I brush my thumb across her lips. "I'm sorry your dream isn't what you thought it would be, *mon délice*."

"I'm sorry you've been lonely since you moved here," she replies before pressing a kiss against my thumb.

Truthfully, I've been lonelier since before I moved here. Philippe and I were nothing more than roommates for a while before we called it, and even before that, I never felt truly fulfilled. But now... "I don't feel so lonely anymore," I say. Noelle's eyes light up, and my heart skips a damn beat.

27

NOELLE

A non-Christmas-themed party in Wintermore is rare, and I should be enjoying myself a lot more, all things considered. I should be celebrating with everyone else; I've busted my ass for weeks for this movie, and it's finally done. The cast and crew are leaving town, and this time next year, they're going to help us put Wintermore back on the map when the movie comes out.

Everyone is excited. Everyone is happy. People are dancing, drinking, and laughing. Uncle Henry is spinning around the makeshift dance floor in the middle of the town hall with Sunny in his arms while Rora watches them, her eyes glittering. Rora at a Wintermore party is cause for celebration in and of itself. My parents are talking to some of the crew, Felix is helping Abigail throw darts against the back wall, Shay is laughing with one of the actresses from the movie, and I'm losing my mind. Because Shay is laughing with one of the actresses from the fucking movie, and I, apparently, have a jealous streak.

I know it has less to do with Shay talking to someone else and more to do with the fact that she apparently refuses to talk to me. Well, talk to me about what I *want* to talk about, anyway. Us.

Not a want, in fact. A need. Because as of last night, we're no longer working together, and I have no idea where things stand. Anytime I try to broach the topic, she shuts down, changes the subject, or distracts me by slipping into the conversation that she isn't wearing underwear… Okay, that was just once, but it did the trick.

It has to be intentional. Every day for the past week, I've mentioned that I wasn't feeling great about the movie wrapping. Initially, Shay took that to mean that I just didn't want to go back to working so much at The Enchanted Bakery—which I don't, and she knows that, which meant it was all too easy for her to distract me by getting me to open up more about what I dislike about my job.

Every time I've brought it up since that conversation—under-wearless incident aside—Shay's gone out of her way to assure me that it's going to work out, that it's okay to take a step back. She's been unbelievably sweet about it, and I'm not sure how to get from her reassuring me to, *actually, the reason I'm so out of sorts is because I'm pretty sure I'm falling in love with you, and I have no idea what to do about that.*

I've never been in love before. I've never been that lucky. And I suppose I can't know for sure that this is that, but it sure feels like how I imagined. Of course, whenever I've imagined it, I pictured something a little less *casual*, a little less *friendly*.

When I think about what I'd like my future partner to be like, Shay ticks every box: kind and caring, family-oriented (even if her brother doesn't feel the same way), passionate about her busi-ness, happy to go out and do things like spur of the moment boat trips, but equally happy to curl up at home and binge cozy TV shows. She doesn't want kids, and neither do I. She's a cat person, and I'm a Croissant person at the very least. She likes ABBA, and I like watching her sing ABBA.

But mostly… she makes everything a little quieter. A little more peaceful, a little brighter, a little better. A lot better, in truth.

I have to try and wrap my head around the possibility that she doesn't want more. If she wants to keep things casual, to keep sleeping together, but never be more, I'll survive. At least I'll still be spending time with her. But there's a chance, however small, that she'll decide to call things off altogether. And I'll somehow have to be okay on the other side of it.

The unknown, as frustrating as it is, is safe, but it's not maintainable. Working together, there was a guarantee of when we'd be seeing each other next. I have no idea where Shay and I will stand as of tomorrow morning.

I watch her, my heart screaming at me to cross the dance floor and just talk to her. She looks amazing, as always. She's wearing a pretty light blue dress with pink flowers. It's strapless, making her locket stand out against the hollow of her throat.

The actress shows Shay something on her phone, and insecurity creeps over me. She's beautiful, yes, but that's not what makes my stomach twist. She's a successful actress who probably doesn't hate her job and has her life together. Sure, I don't know that for certain, but there's one thing I do know: she's closer to Shay's age than I am.

Asking Shay to be in this with me, for real, is asking her to deal with all the downsides of age gap relationships that Rora and Uncle Henry talked about. I would be asking her to deal with the small-town gossip, to come out to her parents and explain not only that she's dating a woman, but that I was born when she was a junior in high school. Her relationship with them is already strained, and I don't want to make it harder.

Maybe the right thing is to walk away, to take the decision out of her hands and call it a day. But I don't want to do that. I don't want to be on the other side of the room watching someone more age-appropriate touching her arm, asking her a question, leading her to… the dance floor.

Oh.

I turn away before I have to watch the woman I'm falling in love with dance with someone who isn't me.

"Fuck." I don't mean to say it as loudly as I guess I do, considering the gasps and shocked looks from the ladies' running club sitting at the table near me. I have to get out of here.

Not waiting to be admonished by the townsfolk who have watched me grow up but failed to accept that I'm a whole-ass grown-up, I flee. A very grown-up thing to do, if you ask me.

I ignore the bang of the door as it closes behind me, taking the town hall steps two at a time until I'm standing in the parking lot. It's quiet out here; everyone else is inside enjoying themselves. I can still hear the music as I walk across the parking lot, gravel crunching beneath my heels.

There aren't a lot of opportunities to get dressed up in Wintermore, and I haven't had the chance to get out of town in a while. I'm not much of a dress person, but tonight… Hell, I dressed up for her.

I've only worn the amber-yellow dress once—my mom and I convinced Rora (begrudgingly) to have a baby shower, and she chose a sunshine theme before any of us knew Sunny's name. The crepe dress is more suited to a spring baby shower than the parking lot outside a fall party, but this is the nicest dress I own. It seems like a waste as I perch on the edge of the bed of my parents' truck, kicking the gravel.

The breeze tickles my hair, and I look up, frowning at the black and gray smudges dotting the sky. The air smells like it does right before a downpour, and, though I appreciate the weather mirroring my demeanor, I'm not dressed for a storm.

If I start walking home now, I might make it before the sky opens, but I don't get the chance to leave before I hear the town hall doors open, and Shay appears in the shadowy doorway. She scans the parking lot, something like relief flickering on her face when she spots me.

"Hey," she calls as she crosses the lot. "Are you okay? You kind of just ran out of there."

"I'm fine," I answer, and Shay stops short of me at my tone.

"You don't sound fine."

"Well, I am," I bite back. "You looked like you were having fun." I don't mean to say it, don't mean it to sound so bitter, and I watch as realization dawns on Shay's face the second the words leave my lips.

"You're upset that I was talking to someone else?" There's no judgment in her tone, but I still deny it immediately.

"No."

She raises a brow, twisting her mouth.

"I'm not upset that you were talking to someone. I'm upset that I should've been the one asking you to dance."

A soft smile lifts Shay's lips, and she takes a deep breath. "Karina—that's her name—didn't ask me to dance."

"But I watched you go onto the dance floor with her."

"Right. Because she was taking me to meet her husband, who was dancing with their daughter. He grew up in Oakland, and she wanted to introduce us," Shay explains, but instead of relief that she wasn't dancing with her, I feel a sudden crash, like the adrenaline that propelled me to bolt from the party is gone in a flash.

Because if it's not Karina, it'll be someone else. For as long as Shay and I are *casual friends*, there could always be someone else.

Stepping down from the truck bed, I rub my face with my hands, finding it hard to care that I'm almost definitely fucking up my makeup.

Shay's only standing six feet away, but it feels like there's a much bigger distance between us, and I can't handle it anymore.

"I can't do this anymore, Shay."

28

SHAY

"**I** can't do this anymore, Shay."

It's funny how six words can split you in two, just like that. Not just the words, but the trembling in Noelle's voice as she says it. I want to cross the space between us and wrap her in my arms, rub away the goosebumps peppering her skin where the cool air is hitting it, forehead-kiss away the pain in her voice. But I'm frozen in place as the words sink in.

"I can't do this anymore, Shay."

"Noelle," I say, the wind carrying the word until it's nothing more than a whispered plea.

"I've been trying to talk to you about this all week," she continues, a dull ache settling in my bones. "You keep distracting me and changing the subject, but we have to talk about it. We can't keep pretending like things aren't going to change now that we're not working together."

She's not wrong. I've been avoiding this conversation like it's my job, changing the subject whenever she brings it up, because I'm not ready to talk about it. But she's also not wrong that we can't keep acting like it's not happening.

The movie is over, and we might very well be over with it.

"Okay," I say, but I'm more choked up than I realize, and it's barely audible. I clear my throat. "Okay. Let's talk."

I take a step toward her, and she takes one toward me, and we meet in the middle of the parking lot. I look up at Noelle on a regular day, but she's wearing heels, so I'm forced to tilt my chin even more to meet her eye. She's blindingly beautiful, a bright spot in an otherwise dreary day.

"I don't even know where to start," she says, and it's killing me that I can't reach out to her.

"I've been dreading this conversation," I admit. "That's why I kept avoiding it. I'd say I'm sorry, but I'm not. I liked being in a bubble with you."

"I did too. But it was easy to stay in a bubble when we had no choice but to be, and now that we're not working together… Bubbles don't last forever."

"No. I suppose they don't," I reply, my voice weak.

Noelle hugs her body, clearly cold, but also making herself smaller, and I hate it. She lets out a shaky breath. "I never wanted to be your friend, Shay. At first, for all the wrong reasons, but after, I didn't want you to be my friend. I just wanted you to be mine."

Everything beyond Noelle and me disappears, and I swear my heart pauses for a moment, just letting her words sink in.

"You wanted…"

"I wanted—I want—you. You kept talking about how things were casual between us, and all I could think about was when I'd be seeing you next." Now that she's started, Noelle's words blend together almost manically. "I've been trying so hard not to push you, but I wanted to take you on dates, bring you to family dinner, talk about a future together. You keep calling it casual, but I think I'm falling in love with you!" The blood drains from Noelle's face, like she didn't mean to say that, but I'm not sure I've ever heard anything sweeter.

Noelle lets out a growl of frustration that's almost a sob. "Fuck, I just… I wanted to ask you to dance."

The last word is swallowed by a rumble of thunder, and the

sky spills down on us. We both look up, and I draw in a deep breath as the rain hits my face. Instantly, the air feels a hundred times clearer, and I'm seeing the whole situation between me and Noelle clearer too—how the hell could I have misinterpreted everything so much? Nico was right. All I had to do was talk to her, and I could've saved us both a lot of stress.

But I was scared, and so was she, and now we're at a crossroads—and I don't plan on taking the wrong road.

"Let's dance," I say, holding my hand out to her. She stares at it, then me, like I've grown a second head.

"I'm sorry—what?"

"You wanted to ask me to dance. So let's dance."

Noelle blinks. "Here? You can feel that it's pouring, right?"

"I can," I say, stepping forward. "And I want to dance with the woman I *know* I'm falling in love with in the pouring rain." It doesn't feel nearly as scary to say it as it did to overthink it; the words feel like exactly what I'm supposed to say, at exactly the right moment, like puzzle pieces slotting into place.

Her lips part, her eyes widening. Raindrops run down her face, smudging her eyeliner, but she's never looked more beautiful than when she steps closer to me. "Shay," she breathes, threading her fingers through mine. She's icy cold as I pull her into me, her yellow dress clinging to her skin. I slowly run one hand down her back, winding it around her waist, holding our clasped hands up.

I look up, and Noelle's eyes are wet from more than just the rain. She presses her forehead to mine, mirroring my position as we sway. The music from the party is barely audible over the rain, but the happy sigh that falls from Noelle's lips is my new favorite soundtrack.

We're drenched, getting more soaked by the second, but I don't care. The moment is perfect, dancing with Noelle in the chilly fall night, her clinging to me as much as I am her—as much as I've wanted to, this whole time. But now, I can.

"This is so much better than in there in front of everyone," she says, laughing as I twirl her and pull right back in.

"It is. Though, for the record, I would dance with you in front of everyone in a heartbeat, *mon délice*," I murmur, and a smile crests Noelle's lips. "I never wanted casual," I say, and she pulls back enough to catch my eye. "I always wanted more—more than I thought we could have, if I'm being honest. But I was scared, and I didn't think you were interested in anything since your life is so hectic."

Noelle worries her bottom lip with her teeth. "It is hectic. That part hasn't changed. I can't promise I'm going to be around as much as I have been while we've been working on the movie, and maybe it's selfish of me to ask you to be with me without being *with* me all the time."

"It's not selfish. It's not like I don't know how busy you are, and, sure, I'm going to miss being with you most of the day, but I understand. I'm okay with it."

"I'm not sure I'm okay with it," she admits. "I know I need to find a better way of doing things so I'm not as miserable all the time, and we can actually spend time together, and I will. Probably not until after the tourist season, though. I understand if you want to wait—"

"I don't," I interrupt. "Time is a precious thing, and I'm not giving up a single second with you."

Noelle's eyes twinkle. "So, say I wanted to ask you to be my girlfriend…"

"I'd say it's too late. I already claimed that title when we started this conversation," I say, and she laughs, a sound so sunshiney, I swear the rain lets up a little.

I spin her around, dipping her. It's not the most elegant, given how much taller than me she is in her heels, but she gasps, placing her hand flat on my chest when I pull her up.

"You're good at this. You've been holding out on me, sweetheart."

"I took dancing lessons when I was younger," I explain.

"Huh. I guess we have a lot to learn about each other. It's a nice thought." Noelle's smile slips a little before she continues, "But I do need to check: are you sure you're okay with our age gap?"

"I'm sure," I confirm. It's not like I've forgotten about it completely, but I think about it a lot less when we're together than I did a few weeks ago.

"A hundred percent? Because I understand why you're hesitant. It's not always going to be easy."

"I know that."

"People will judge us," she continues. "They're going to talk about us behind our backs. And to our faces, probably. I've been with Rora and my uncle Henry, and I've seen people mistake him for her dad."

"Are you trying to convince me to change my mind?" I ask, joking mostly, but she shakes her head quickly.

"No. No, of course not. I just want to make sure you're comfortable with everything," she says, rushing her words together.

"I am. I promise. Like you said, it's not always going to be easy, but I don't care what people say about us. Do you?"

She wrinkles her nose. "Of course I don't."

"Well, then. Now that we have that out of the way…" I clasp her face between my hands, brushing the tip of her nose with mine. "Hi."

"Hi."

"I'd like to kiss my girlfriend in the rain now, if that's okay with you."

Noelle doesn't answer with words. Capturing my lips, she slips her tongue between them, groaning as she drinks me in. She tastes like all of my favorite flavors in one place.

She tastes like… mine.

29

NOELLE

"You have got to be kidding me. We just finished a month of almost constant baking, and this is what you want to do on our first real day off?" I stare at Shay in disbelief.

Here I was thinking that we'd have a slow, lazy morning after the wrap party—after Shay cemented her hold on my heart in the pouring rain, dancing to the distant sounds of *Monster Mash,* of all things. Preferably a lazy morning in bed, with no clothes. But Shay's side of the bed was empty when I woke up—almost empty, anyway. Croissant had the same idea as me about the lazy morning.

No part of me thought Shay would want to bake.

"I'm not meeting your family empty-handed," she says, inspecting an apple before tossing it in a bowl to wash.

"You're not meeting my family at all. You met them years ago."

"Not as your girlfriend," she points out, and I melt.

"That's true." I step closer to her, and she tugs me in, wrapping her arms around me and leaning in to kiss the tip of my nose. *Girlfriend.* It's more than I let myself hope for, even though it's all I've thought about since I peeled her clothes off in the basement kitchen.

"Good morning," she murmurs against my lips.

"Morning. You're not nervous about tonight, are you?"

"A little, I guess. I know you said your parents are cool with it, but I haven't officially done the "meet the parents" thing since I was in my twenties. And Rora scares me a little."

I snort, because Rora is, without a doubt, the most intimidating person in the family. "It'll be good, I promise. Everyone is going to love you, including Rora." Including me, I want to say, but thankfully, my brain isn't totally useless before caffeine. Jumping from girlfriend to *I love you, please stay with me forever*, in less than twenty-four hours, is a little too eager.

We both said we were falling for each other, not that we loved each other. But the second I realized she feels the same way about me as I do her, falling turned to fallen real fast. It's like my heart was just waiting for my anxiety to scoot out of the way and let my head get on board.

Right now, I want to get on *Shay*. In her bedroom.

"You know, I keep cookie dough in my freezer. We don't have to make anything from scratch," I say, trying with all my might to pull her back to bed.

She doesn't budge, laughing softly. "I like baking. And I like baking with you," she specifies. "Seriously, *mon délice*, when was the last time you baked for fun?"

I can't answer that, and she knows it. It's been over a year, at least.

"Fine," I relent with an overexaggerated sigh. "What are we making?"

"Apple and amaretto caramel pie with cardamom whipped cream," she answers, and my mouth waters. I've never been the biggest almond person, but Shay does things with them that I can't describe. I've yet to taste something she's made that I don't love.

"Put me to work, Chef," I say, grabbing the spare apron she has hanging over the back of a chair.

Shay chuckles and swats my ass with a spatula before handing me an apple peeler.

I make quick work of the apples, snacking on the peel and feeding some to Shay. The nicer, twirlier pieces, we save for a garnish. When the apples are peeled, I take a break to make us coffee, then thinly slice them while Shay makes the pie filling. The whole thing comes together in twenty minutes, and I'm surprised by how much I enjoy baking with no purpose beyond having something delicious to share with the people I love.

And watching Shay bake has become somewhat of a favorite pastime of mine. Move over *Grey's* and *Gilmore Girls*—there's a new show in town, and I'm hooked.

She starts the whipped cream in her stand mixer until it forms soft peaks, then unhooks the bowl, because she likes to finish it by hand in case she overwhips it.

I sip my coffee and enjoy the view as she works. There are a lot of differences in how Shay and I work—her in disarray, me with order—but the most striking is how happy she always looks when she's baking. There's a light in her eyes that fizzled out of mine the second I made a job of this. A light I'd love to get back.

It's a naive thought, perhaps, that I could find it again with Shay. Baking is less stressful when she's in my general vicinity, but I'm still always running through mental checklists of things to do for the bakery that aren't baking. It takes me out of the peace that measuring and weighing and folding ingredients usually brings me.

The last thing I want to do is be taken out of the moment with Shay.

She opens a drawer and pulls out the first thing her fingers touch—a mini whisk, no longer than seven inches from the tip of the wires to the end of the handle. Shay notices me eyeing it dubiously.

"I know, I know. It's absolutely useless and I never use it. I only bought it because it was small, and small things are cute."

I snort, stepping closer as she swipes a dollop of the cardamom cream with the wires and holds it out to me. The instant I close my lips around the cream, my eyes flutter closed, and a moan slips from my lips.

"Holy shit, sweetheart. This is incredible. I want to put it on everything," I say, licking the last of the cream from the whisk.

A rosy pink blush colors Shay's cheeks.

I rake my gaze over her. "What are you thinking about?" I ask, edging closer to her.

Shay swallows, drawing her lips between her teeth. Her pupils flare, swallowing the smoky gray of her irises. "Uh… nothing."

Her whole face is flaming now, and I have to fight not to chuckle. I close in on her, backing her up against the counter. She groans as I press my body into hers.

"Are you thinking about me putting the cream everywhere, sweetheart?"

She nods, her breath coming in short, ragged bursts. I take the whisk from her hand.

"Question."

"Yeah?"

"How mad will you be if I ruin this batch of cream so we can't use it for the pie?"

"Please ruin it. We can make more," she begs.

Well, she doesn't have to ask me twice. I load the whisk up with cream and deposit a spot on her nose. Shay chuckles as I lean in and swipe it with my tongue.

"Not what I thought you meant by everywhere."

"Patience, sweetheart." I drag the whisk across her lips and kiss the cream off. "We're getting there."

The vanilla and cardamom taste even better mingled with the

taste of her tongue. Shay tugs the scrunchie from my hair, and I moan as her nails scrape against my scalp.

I practically tear her clothes off. Part of me wants to take her to bed so we have more space, but the thought of the cleanup… No, the kitchen will do. It's not a big kitchen, and there's very little counter space since she has two stand mixers, a coffee machine, and a fancy toaster oven. But she also has a dining table that looks pretty steady.

"How strong is your dining table?"

"Pretty strong, I guess? Nico made it."

That's enough for me; as little as Nico is known, he's known for his woodworking skills.

I nudge her toward the table, grabbing the bowl with the cream and the mini whisk. Setting it down, I lift Shay until she's sitting on the table.

"Lie back, sweetheart."

She obliges instantly. The table isn't quite long enough, so her feet dangle off the end a little, but I fully intend to be lifting them anyway.

I grab a pillow from the couch and place it under her head, leaning down to brush a light kiss over her lips before I stand back and survey the scene before me. She's naked, save for her locket, and her chest is flushed, rising and falling rapidly, her fingers twitching in my direction, like she's struggling not to reach for me.

"You're so beautiful," I murmur, running my fingers down her torso. Shay sighs contentedly, her eyes closing, any lingering tension dissolving from her body.

It gives me the perfect opportunity to pick up the cream-covered whisk and drag it all over her body. Shay gasps, her eyes flying open as the cool metal wires and chilled cream touch her skin.

I paint her like a canvas, strokes of white with black vanilla and cardamom sprinkles. Shay always looks like a work of art, but I like making my mark on her, even if only temporarily.

I grab the scrunchie she pulled from my hair and throw it back up, because I don't plan on having time to wash my hair before family dinner, and I'm not sure showing up covered in cream would do anything to put Shay at ease. With that in mind, I also strip off my clothes while she watches me, hungrily.

As soon as I'm naked, I pounce on her, running my tongue over every inch of her, devouring both Shay and the cream. She's so fucking sweet, and the cream really is the cherry on top. Every little whimper that spills from her lips, every sigh of my name, feels like a goddamn sugar rush.

I run my tongue over her tattoo, licking the last of the cream. Shay watches me clean off the whisk with my tongue, warming up the metal, before I drag it across her nipple. She cries out, her back bowing.

"*Please,* baby," she whimpers as I replace the whisk with my tongue, alternating my mouth with the whisk until she's trembling. "*Tu me donnes l'impression d'être au paradis. Encore. S'il te plaît.*"

I know enough French to know she's begging for more, and I'm powerless to say no to her when she's speaking English, let alone when she speaks French.

I take pity on her, dragging both myself and the whisk down her body, settling between her legs. I could take it slow, tease her a little more, but she's already so on edge, and I haven't gotten enough of the taste of her. Her legs are already parted for me, but I lift them so they're sitting on my shoulders, lean in, and roll her clit between my lips. She's fucking soaked, and I press two fingers inside her, curling them and pressing against her G-spot.

Shay tightens around my fingers, her legs pressing against my head, moving her hips like she needs more. I pull back enough to glance toward the bedroom. Shay might be a bigger fan of my toy collection than I am—so much so that I now keep half of it here. I have sex toys at her apartment before a toothbrush.

But I don't want to leave her to go and get them. I've almost resigned myself to do just that when my eyes fall on the whisk sitting discarded on the table.

Beyond both of us running out of patience, there's a reason I didn't bring the whipped cream lower; there are just some things that shouldn't go in vaginas, and sugar is one of them. But the handle… It's the perfect size and shape, smooth black plastic, and entirely cream-free.

I pull my fingers out of her, and Shay lifts herself up on her elbows to protest, but the protest fades into nothing as she watches me pick the whisk up and run the handle between her lips. She moans, her eyes wide.

"What do you reckon?" I ask, teasing her entrance with the handle of the whisk. The metal wires are sticky in my grip, but I barely notice as Shay nods, pushing her body closer to mine.

"God, yes," she says, and I laugh at her urgency.

I press the handle inside her slowly, testing it—it feels smooth, but I don't want to hurt her—watching it disappear, salivating. I stop before the wires are touching her, going completely still, and Shay cries in frustration.

"*Please*. I want you to fuck me, *mon délice*."

Fuck, her accent when she speaks French drives me wild. And how could I possibly refuse a request like that?

She looks incredible with the whisk inside her, and I can't take my eyes off her pussy as I pull the handle out and press it back inside her, ramping up the speed. I'll never be able to use a whisk again without remembering how good it feels to fuck her, how sweet the sounds of her breaking apart are.

I bend my head to lick her clit again, alternating fast and slow, gentle licks, cool breaths, and light brushes of my teeth, and a few minutes later, Shay goes completely still and silent for a split second. And then she's shaking, twisting on the table, chanting my name like a prayer as she comes.

I drink every drop of her in, every sound, savoring her, forgetting for a moment that I no longer have to worry about every time being the last time—every taste being the last taste. She's mine, and I'm hers, and we can do this whenever we want.

The thought should calm me down, but it does exactly the opposite. Shay is almost through the orgasm, but I'm not ready to let it go. I angle the whisk, pressing the end of the handle firmly against her G-spot, and press her clit between my lips, sucking until she gasps. The second wave seems to catch her by surprise. It's quieter, her mouth dropping open, but no sounds escape her. Her hips jump from the table as I massage her G-spot with the handle, pulling it out just in time for her to squirt all over me.

Oh shit, I already know I'm going to get addicted to this.

Like she's lost control of her body, Shay's thighs twitch and tremble. She pants, and I let her legs down gently, leaning over her body to kiss her. Every inch of her body is scarlet—and a little sticky, and I love it.

"You did so good, sweetheart," I murmur against her lips.

She opens her mouth to answer, but all that comes out is a sigh.

I chuckle, standing up and making eye contact as I pick up the whisk and clean off the handle. Shay's eyes get somehow darker—charcoal gray, and ravenous.

She sits up, and I'm honestly surprised she has the energy. She reaches for me, and I lean until I'm close enough for her to grip my chin and pull my lips to hers. The kiss she lays on me is desperate—fiery. My heart pounds against my rib cage, electricity shocking me all over.

We break apart, both sticky messes fighting to fill our lungs with air, but Shay holds me to her, biting my bottom lip, and whispering, "My turn."

30

SHAY

Before Georgie died, I like to think we were a close family. I have a big extended family on my dad's side, and we had Harland dinners, vacations, and game nights. It was a good way to grow up.

After Georgie died, no one could face it. Part of me still wonders if no one could face *me* and how much I look like her, but, regardless of the reason, there were no more dinners, vacations, or game nights.

When I married Philippe, the Moore family was much more formal than I was used to growing up. Their dinners were stuffy, and I never felt quite at home. I never felt like a Moore. Which I wasn't, to be fair—I never changed my name, something I was grateful for after the divorce. One less thing to deal with.

Needless to say, it's been a while since I had a family dinner that wasn't reserved. But I can tell within ten seconds of walking into Noelle's parents' house that the Whittens don't have that problem.

They greet me like they would anytime I see them around town, with welcome smiles and a warm aura. It explains so much about who Noelle is that this is the family she was raised in. Noelle squeezes my hand as her mom, Kate, tells me how happy they are to have me, and I feel some of the knots in my chest loosen.

Rora and Henry arrive just after us, with Sunny hanging out in a carrier on her dad's chest.

"Hi, Shay. It's good to see you," Henry says with a glowing smile.

Rora lifts a hand to wave beside him. "Hey."

I wasn't kidding when I told Noelle that Rora scares me. Unlike the Whittens, she's not a smiley person. She has a reputation in Wintermore for being "a bit of a Grinch." Which is to say, she doesn't like Christmas, and she's not big on people—and she doesn't feel the need to pretend otherwise. It's admirable, really, and I like her a lot, even if she scares me.

She runs her gaze down until it catches on Noelle's and my clasped hands, and something in her expression softens.

"Enough of the introductions. I think you know what I'm going to ask," Noelle says, looking at Henry.

He shakes his head, but he's smiling as he unclips the baby carrier. "'Ask' implies that you don't usually demand," he says, kissing his daughter's head and handing her over.

Noelle squeezes my hand once more before dropping it so she can take Sunny, her face lighting up. "Hi, Sunny girl." She bounces her, and Sunny flashes a toothless smile. She looks over at me, curiously. "You remember Shay, don't you? I suppose we have you and your dating app antics to thank for this, actually," Noelle points out.

"Hi, Sunny," I say softly. She reaches for me, and I offer her my finger, which she immediately squeezes in her little fist.

"That's her version of a stamp of approval," Henry tells me.

Thank god. Sunny not liking me would be a dealbreaker, I think.

I'm not a big baby person—kids, sure, but babies can't talk, and I'm never sure what to do with them. Noelle looks cute with Sunny, though, chatting away like the four-month-old might start talking back.

Noelle told me everyone would be dressed casually for family dinner, but I've been burned before, so I made her pick something out for me. She picked jeans and a burgundy sweater, and I fit right in—Kate and Felix are both wearing Christmas sweaters, which doesn't surprise me. Neither does the Christmas tree in the living room, bigger even than Noelle's. Truthfully, I'd expect nothing less from the Whitten family.

Rora notices me looking at the tree and says, "So, Shay. Thoughts on Christmas?"

Everyone turns their full attention to me, even Sunny. You could hear a pin drop—or a pine needle, I suppose, to stay on theme.

I glance sideways at Noelle. "I… like it?" She wrinkles her nose. "But I don't come from a big Christmas family, so I'm sure I'll learn to love it."

Noelle's lips lift, and, if I do say so myself, I'm passing the Whitten family tests with flying colors. Well, for most of them.

Rora groans. "Damn it. I hoped I might finally have an ally here."

"You never know—Sunny might grow up to be a Grinch," Noelle suggests, and her dad, Charlie, glares at her.

"Don't even put that out there. Not that we don't love you, Ror, even though you hate everything this family stands for," he says, patting Rora on the shoulder.

"I love you too," she replies, rolling her eyes.

I know Charlie isn't actually Rora's dad, but from what Noelle has told me, he may as well be, and I can see it. The interaction is so reminiscent of how my dad used to act with me and Georgie. All of this is so reminiscent of *before*. This is what family used to feel like for me—what it could feel like again, here, with the Whittens. It's comfortable and homey, and I don't feel out of place. Sure, it's not technically my first time meeting any of the Whittens, but being in their home is a lot different from running into Kate at the grocery store or Charlie spotting me lugging sacks of flour from my trunk and offering a hand. I don't know any of them, not really.

But I could. I could have people here. For so long, it felt so far out of reach, but I never could have guessed that I'd fall for Noelle.

Fallen, not falling. I might not have spoken the words yet, but I feel them all the same.

I startle as Noelle touches my knee.

"Hey. You okay, sweetheart?" she asks softly, and I realize she's no longer holding Sunny. Shit, how long did I disappear into my head for?

"Yeah, of course. Sorry, I just zoned out." Noelle doesn't look convinced, so I cover her hand with mine and add, "I really like it here. With your family."

Understanding crests Noelle's ocean eyes. She just gets me, like it's some inherent, natural thing. She brings our joint hands to her lips and presses a soft, searing kiss against my skin. "I like having you here. We all do. On that note, don't be alarmed if my mom asks you for your size for Christmas PJs later," she warns, and I chuckle. Only here would I be warned about something like that.

I can see where Noelle got her love of food; both of her parents are incredible in the kitchen. I've been to Italy half a dozen times at least, but I've never had pasta this good: pumpkin and sage ravioli, with a creamy brown butter garlic sauce and maple-glazed walnuts, and rosemary olive focaccia—Felix's addition. It's divine.

We finish with Noelle's and my pie, and a fresh bowl of

cardamom whipped cream. It's a perfect pairing, and everyone digs in happily.

"Should we feel bad that we're the only ones who didn't make and bring something?" Henry asks Rora as she spoons extra cream on top of her apple pie.

"We brought Sunny," she answers with a shrug.

Sunny is sitting on Felix's lap while he eats dessert, babbling up at him. Of all the Whittens, I know Felix the least. Mostly, I know what Noelle has told me, and he's not what I expected. He, Rora, and Noelle bicker almost constantly, and he comes across as someone who doesn't take much seriously, but he's so soft with Sunny, he made a perfect focaccia from scratch, and he set the table without being asked, with napkins folded to look like bows and everything.

He and Noelle look alike, though Felix has Kate's soft hazel eyes. In some lights, they look green like Rora's, in others, they're a warm brown. Eyes aside, Noelle and Felix are unmistakably siblings. Their mannerisms are identical, from the way they eat left to right across their plates, to the way they light up from head to toe when they laugh.

It's the same way Charlie laughs; it's easy to see that they're a patchwork of their parents.

"That was damn good," Charlie says, finishing the last bit of his pie. Charlie, Kate, and Henry all grew up in Texas, and Noelle and Felix lived there for a good few years before moving to Wyoming. It's been more than twenty years since they moved here, but Charlie and Henry still have a strong southern drawl. Kate has all but lost the twang, and Felix and Noelle only have it on certain words—it's stronger when they're around their dad and uncle, though.

"Thanks, Dad," Noelle says, barely fighting a yawn. "Shay gets all the credit, though. I was going to bring cookies from the freezer."

"They would still have been delicious," I chime in, and she glows.

"So," Charlie continues, just as I take a sip of my lemonade. "Shay. What exactly are your intentions with our daughter?"

I almost spit out my drink.

"Dad!" Noelle immediately shouts, aghast. "What the hell? No. We're not doing this."

"But honey, we didn't get to do it with Rora," Kate says. "This is our only chance."

"Yeah, we all knew exactly what Uncle Henry's inten—hey!" Felix protests as Rora balls up her napkin and throws it, hitting him square in the face.

"What was that about intentions?"

Henry clears his throat, interrupting before they start fighting. "Personally, I don't think we need to subscribe to that kind of patriarchal bullshit, anyway."

Rora looks at him like he's just stripped naked in front of her, and I get it; Henry's not my type, but feminism is hot.

I put my hand on Noelle's knee, and she automatically snuggles closer to me.

"Since Noelle and I have officially been together for about"—I look at the mistletoe clock above the kitchen door—"twenty hours, we haven't had much time to talk about that kind of thing. But I guess right now, my intention is to do what I can to take some of the stress off her shoulders and help her through the holiday season—as much as she'll let me, anyway."

I look around the table to gauge the reaction, and Rora actually looks impressed. Thank god.

Kate sighs. "Damn. That was a great answer. How are we supposed to interrogate you now?"

"You're not, Mom." Noelle's eyes crinkle when she looks at me. "It was a great answer, sweetheart."

Suddenly, I can't wait to get her home and in my arms. I love being here, but I miss holding her.

Felix pushes back from the table and stands, Sunny perched on his arm. "Who's ready to get their A-S-S beat at Monopoly? Sunny's on my team."

31

NOELLE

I dream of sugar, to-do lists, dirty dishes, and cinnamon-scented smoke, a blaring alarm, and someone shouting my name, and—

"Noelle. Wake up."

I wake with a start, Shay shaking my shoulders. Her eyes are wide, and she has her T-shirt pulled up over her mouth. It only takes me a single inhale to realize why—the smoke wasn't a dream.

"Where?" I choke out before covering my mouth. My bedroom isn't visibly smoky, but I can feel it.

"Downstairs, I think."

The bakery. Shit.

Unlike Shay's apartment, which is accessed by stairs outside, my stairway is directly connected to the bakery. When I first moved in, I thought that was a perk, to be able to go from my bed to work without going outside, but the convenience quickly became cloying when I realized it felt like I was always at work. I didn't consider the safety concerns.

We move like we're in double-speed, pulling on pants and shoes, trying not to breathe in the smoke. Thank god we left Croissant sleeping at Shay's last night—I can't imagine trying to wrangle a scared cat right now. As it is, I barely manage to grab my phone before Shay pulls me out of the bedroom.

My living room is smokier, but nothing prepares us for the stairwell. Shay wrenches the door open, and we both jump back as a wall of heat and thick smoke assaults us. This is not the time to panic—I need all the air I can get—but that doesn't stop my heart from racing a mile a minute.

I pull Shay back from the doorway so I can speak without inhaling too much smoke.

"We either make a run for it down the stairs to the fire exit, or we try to climb over the balcony and hope the store's awning holds us." It's not the biggest drop in the world, but I don't like the idea of falling.

Shay peers down the stairs. "It's dark—the fire isn't in the stairwell yet, but we don't know if the awning is damaged."

"Right. Shit." Something about the "yet" in her sentence makes a wave of panic course through me. Fuck.

She must notice the way I freeze up, and she squeezes my hand. "We've got this, baby. It's just a few stairs and we're outside."

I nod, because what else is there to do here?

"I'll go first. Hold on to the back of my T-shirt," Shay says, and I know better than to waste time arguing over who goes first.

The air quality in the apartment is bad, but the stairs are worse, so we both take deep breaths before covering our faces. My lungs scream, burning as I breathe in the thick air, but there's no time to think about it. We approach the door, and Shay drops my hand so I can grab her T-shirt.

And we run. As carefully and quickly as we can, holding our breaths. It probably doesn't take us more than thirty seconds to get down the stairs, but I've never felt heat like this, emanating from the door that leads into the bakery. I glance back at it as Shay presses the bar on the fire exit door and tugs me out into the cool night.

The door bangs closed behind us, and I suck in a long breath of cool mountain air. Which, apparently, is the wrong thing to do, because it catches in my throat and I have to lean against the dumpster to stay upright as a coughing fit overtakes me. My mouth tastes like ash.

Shay must have had the same idea as me, because she's coughing up a storm, too. I reach for her as mine subside, clasping her face.

"Are you okay, sweetheart? Tell me you're okay."

She presses her hand against mine, closing her eyes as she stops coughing. "I'm okay. We're okay."

We stand for a moment, just holding each other. From here, the building doesn't look different, save for the black smoke coiling above it.

A siren sounds in the distance, and we break apart.

"We should probably go around front so they know we're okay," Shay says, and I nod, because if I talk, I might start coughing again.

I follow Shay around the side of the building, grateful for the alleyways on either side of the bakery. Hopefully nothing else catches. She gasps as we step onto the street, and I follow her line of sight.

I almost don't believe what I'm seeing. Not my bakery, that's for sure. It's barely visible. The whole storefront is a mass of orange, yellow, and red, and it's a good thing we didn't try to climb down to the awning, because it's gone.

The pumpkin window display I woke up at four a.m. to put up—gone. The candy-cane-striped paint around the door I spent hours getting perfect—gone. The gilded store sign that I designed in my room when I was fifteen and cried when I saw it brought to life—gone.

Shay pulls me back so we're further from the fire. I hear the firetrucks stopping, their doors banging, and someone shouting my name—Quinn, probably. He's the chief of Wintermore's volunteer fire department, which means my family is probably on the way. Maybe it's my parents' tires I hear squealing, their car doors I hear slamming.

But I can't focus on any of that.

All I can think about is everything I've ever worked for, burning down before my eyes.

And the deep, bone-crushing relief I feel at the sight of it.

SHAY

Considering how little experience they get in Wintermore, the volunteer fire department has the fire out in twenty-five minutes. It all goes fairly smoothly, and once the fire is out, a few of the team go in to check for lingering embers.

From the street, it's hard to say how much damage there is, but I saw the look Quinn exchanged with Felix when he first checked out the bakery. It's not good.

The Whittens arrived almost as quickly as the fire department. Noelle accepted the hugs but didn't speak to anyone other than Rora—I watched Noelle ask her a question, but I was swept up by the Whittens, hugging me and checking to make sure I was okay.

Just seven hours ago, we were laughing at Charlie's blatant attempt to cheat at Monopoly. It's scary how quickly things change, but I can't pretend I'm not touched at how easily the Whittens have accepted me in their midst—they seem genuinely concerned for me.

Noelle insisted I get checked out first. I feel fine, but Quinn told us it was protocol, and Noelle practically pushed me in his direction. He checked my vitals, and other than a strong smell of smoke and a lingering cough he assured me was normal, I got the all clear.

Despite her insistence that I get checked out, he practically had to drag Noelle to get looked over. I hover by her family, tuning out their theories on what caused the fire, watching her. Quinn doesn't look worried, thank god. But I'm less concerned about the physical impact of the fire than I am about how Noelle is going to react to having her dream go up in flames.

Quinn gives her a blanket, and she wraps it around her shoulders, staring up at the charred remains of the bakery as he walks in our direction.

"She's okay," he says to a collective sigh of relief. "I think she just needs a minute to herself."

He heads back to help in the bakery, and I turn back to face Noelle. I've never wished I could read her mind more. Her expression is unreadable, almost blank. I'm not sure I've ever seen her so… switched off.

"You okay?" Rora nudges me lightly, stealing my attention from Noelle.

"Yeah," I answer on autopilot, but Rora gives me a skeptical expression. "I am, I just… God, that could've been so much worse, you know?"

"I know. I'm so glad you're both okay. Thank you for getting her out, Shay."

"Do you think she's okay?"

Rora wrinkles her nose, blowing out a long breath. "She's… recalibrating. She has a lot to think about, and it's been a long time coming, but these are shitty circumstances to force her into it. She'll be okay, though. She's Noelle—where some people come out of hard things tarnished, she shows up brighter, every time."

"She really is like a little ray of sunshine," I agree, and Rora chuckles.

"Why do you think Sunny's middle name is Noelle?"

Before I get a chance to answer, an engine rumbles along the street, and I have to give myself a shake as I watch a figure exit the truck.

Rora stands on her tiptoes beside me to look. "Is that—"

"Nico," I say, taking long strides across the asphalt to reach him, because he hasn't spotted me, but he's looking at the wreckage of Noelle's bakery with a terrified expression.

I call his name, and before he even turns, his body sags in what can only be relief.

"You're okay?"

"I'm okay," I confirm. "How did you…" I trail off, because of course he knew something had happened. No matter how distant he's become over the years, we still have the same connection we've always had.

"I woke up and I just knew something was wrong," he confirms, shaking his head. He looks at the charred bakery and curses softly. "Noelle's bakery?"

"Yeah. Her smoke alarm woke me up, but by the time we got outside, it was already pretty far gone."

Nico's eyes widen. "You were inside?"

"The fire never reached her apartment," I assure him. "We've been checked over by the fire chief and EMT, and he's not worried."

"Good. Shit." He rubs his face with his hands. Nico has never been a good sleeper, even before the accident, and I know he would never admit how little he sleeps these days, but the smudges beneath his eyes look almost like bruises. "That's good."

"Are you okay?" I ask gently, even though I know he's not. If the situation were reversed, and I'd gone running into something not knowing if he was okay, I don't know what I'd do, but I know I wouldn't be okay. It's scary enough knowing he's all alone on the mountain.

Instead, he pulls me into a crushing hug.

I squeak because I wasn't expecting it, and I don't remember the last time Nico hugged me. I lean into it; he feels like a home I haven't visited in a long time—familiar, but foreign.

"If something happened to you, Shay—"

"But it didn't."

"But if it *did*," he insists. "I'm going to need you to outlive me, because I can't handle losing you." The "too" is unspoken, but blaring. It has the power to choke me if I let it, but I can't keep letting it.

"That's really morbid. And unfair. Why do I have to be the one to live with it?"

Nico nods behind me, and I look over my shoulder to see Noelle's family huddled around, talking to a firefighter I vaguely recognize—I think he works at the gas station.

"You have people," Nico says.

"I barely know them." Though it doesn't feel like that.

"For now, but you're going to. Right?"

"I hope so. You know, you could have people, too. You could start by taking Bryan up on one of his many offers to visit," I point out, and he gapes at me.

"Seriously? You're almost in a fire, and somehow still finding a way to worry about me?" At least he didn't shoot down the suggestion immediately, for once.

I shrug. "I always worry about you. Just like I assume you always worry about me. I think that's just how family works."

"Maybe. Speaking of family, where's your girl?"

My girl. I like the sound of that.

I point in Noelle's direction, and Nico hums.

"She's younger than I remember."

"She's thirty, it's not that—" I protest until I realize his mustache is twitching. "Shut up."

"You look happy," he says, and he sounds relieved.

"I am. Just worried about how she's going to handle this." I gesture to the general chaos of Main Street.

"She's got good people around her—you included. All you can do is be there for her."

I raise a brow at Nico, because that's weirdly good advice, considering how removed from people he is.

"And on that note," he continues, "go be with her. She's sitting on her own."

I look over at her, still huddled in a blanket on the back of the fire truck, watching everything pass her by.

"She wants space."

"I'm no expert, but she keeps looking over here when you're not looking. I think she probably wants you," Nico says, and, sure enough, Noelle looks up and catches my gaze on her. Even from here, I can tell her face is pale, whether from the chill in the air or the shock, I don't know.

"Do you want to meet her? You know, like, as my girlfriend," I ask Nico, and he doesn't seem surprised by me calling her my girlfriend. I suppose finding me with her family painted a pretty clear picture.

"Of course I do. Just maybe not when she's had probably the most stressful night of her life." Nico's smiles never quite meet his eyes, but he gives me one all the same. "Maybe I could come back down in a few weeks when things are settled?"

Hope swells in my chest, though I know better than to let it get its claws in me. Still, I nod. "I'd love that."

"Right. It's a plan." For a moment, I think he's going to hug me again, but he takes a step back. "I'll call you tomorrow to check in, once you've caught up on sleep."

Call, not text. I don't know what exactly it means, but it feels like progress.

"Sounds good. Thank you for coming."

"Always, Shay. Love you."

"Love you."

I watch him drive away, my heart hammering in my chest. Progress. Definitely progress.

My feet are freezing as I make my way over to Noelle. We didn't have time to put socks on, and the adrenaline that kept me warm has long gone.

She doesn't seem to hear me approach, lost in her own world.

"Hey," I murmur, and she looks up, a little startled. "You want some company?"

I half expect her to decline, to push me away—not because she doesn't want me around, but because she doesn't want to put any of her worries on me. But a soft smile appears on her face, and I take the first deep breath I've taken since we got out of the building.

"From you? Forever," she says, her voice scratchy.

She holds her arm out so I can sit beside her, then pulls the blanket around us both. I loop my arms around her waist, and she rests her chin on the top of my head.

"I'm so sorry," I say, tightening my hold on her as we watch the firefighters doing whatever it is they do when they put a fire out. Quinn had what looked like a checklist when I last saw him.

"Thank you," she replies. "But it's okay."

She sounds… oddly fine. I pull back enough to search her face, and there's a lot less stress than I expected.

Laughing at my scrutiny, Noelle shrugs. "I know it sounds stupid, but it is okay. I promise."

"But you worked so hard to make this place what it was."

"I did, and my hard work paid off, even if just for a little while. My whole life, I've always known exactly what I wanted my future to look like, and I made that happen after busting my ass for years. And then it only took an hour for the universe to more or less wipe the slate clean. For the first time ever, I have absolutely no idea what I'm going to do." Her smile grows wider and brighter with every word, light shining in her eyes, despite the dark night.

"And that's a good thing?" I ask, because it shouldn't sound like one, but it does, how she says it.

"It's a great thing, sweetheart," she confirms. "You know, if this had happened a couple of months ago, I would probably have been catatonic. But I guess somewhere between our first kiss in the kitchen and watching you beat my whole family at Monopoly last night, I figured out there was more to life than a damn bakery." She taps my nose with her finger, then gently cups my chin. "Thank you. Both for getting me out of the fire and reminding me of how good it feels to actually live my life, instead of just existing."

"That's funny," I reply, blinking as tears threaten my eyes. "That sounds a lot like what you've done for me, too."

"Well, that must mean we're meant to be."

"Obviously."

Our happy smiles should feel out of place among the wreckage, but outside of Noelle and me, I'm not paying attention to anything else.

Noelle hops down from the truck and folds the blanket into a rough pile. "I know we have a lot to talk about tomorrow—whatever that intense conversation you and Nico were having was about, what caused the fire, what comes next... but right now, I just want to cuddle in your bed with Croissant, and shut it all out for a few hours."

I take her offered hand—the jump down is further for me—and plant a kiss on her cheek when my feet are flat on the ground again.

"Then let's go home, baby."

33

NOELLE

I smell winter in the air. It's only mid-October, but Wintermore favors its namesake, and fall always feels like it's gone in a flash. Barely three weeks have passed since Shay and I came to the reservoir for our picnic, but the day couldn't be more different: the sky is a cloudy, icy white, and it's cold enough that I pulled a thick sweater from the bin of winter clothes I keep in my parents' garage.

Though there are no structural issues with my apartment, Quinn recommended I give it a few days to air out before moving back in. He got a bunch of stuff out from a list I gave him and politely didn't mention my strap-on wall art or my butt plug Christmas tree.

Wintermore isn't the only thing that's changed as the last of the leaves has fallen from the trees. I feel like a completely different person. Last year, opening the bakery changed me in ways I could never have predicted—I've been impatient, exhausted, uncompromising, and all around unhappy.

"They've lost their tinsel," Mamaw Whitten used to say, instead of "lost their spark."

And that's exactly what I did. I lost my damn tinsel.

It's been happening for longer than I realized, I think. The longer I stayed at the toy store, doing a job I never signed up for, a job I never wanted. I probably would have stuck it out longer if

I hadn't watched Rora make all of her dreams come true as a photographer last year; I was happy for her, but I was so jealous. It was the jealousy that pushed me to say enough was enough. I refused to resent Rora for living her dream, and I refused to let Felix hold me back from mine. The bakery became available, and I told him plainly he could either step up or give up the toy store, but either way, I was leaving.

Of course, Rora was pretty miserable living her dream, jetting all over the world, when all she wanted was to be with my uncle Henry. And I was miserable by day three of owning the bakery.

Felix is thriving. Naturally.

"Can I ask you something?" I whispered to Rora so no one would overhear us yesterday, standing outside the burning bakery.

"Of course."

"When you found out you were pregnant, and you knew you'd have to cut back on traveling—even though it's what you've always wanted to do—were you…"

"Relieved? God, yes. Chasing your dreams isn't a life sentence, Noelle. If you don't like how it feels when you're living it, you can change the dream."

"But baking is all I've ever dreamed of."

"So bake. My dreams changed when I met Henry, when I got pregnant. I still want to travel, but I want to do it with them. You can still bake without owning a bakery you're not happy in."

She made it sound so simple. But maybe it is. It's hard to imagine who I could be without the dream I've been clinging to for the best part of thirty years, but wouldn't it be fun to find out?

The thought of my life burning to the ground, of being forced to start from scratch, should be devastating. But I've spent so long toiling over my feelings for the bakery—the resentment, the guilt, the disappointment. Something about breathing in the smoke and watching the source of those feelings burn made everything so much clearer.

I look up as Shay drops a blanket around my shoulders and sits in the spot beside me.

"How did you get here before me when I drove?"

"Long legs," I reply, passing her a cup from The Frosty Bean. I was ready before her this morning, so I decided to walk to pick up coffee and meet here. Living in Wintermore, it's easy to take the fresh mountain air for granted, but I've found myself wanting to spend more time outside since the fire.

"They're good legs," Shay says before sipping the peppermint mocha and sighing. She hums at the taste. "It's like Christmas in a cup." She squints up at the gray sky. "It's starting to look like it, too. I swear it feels like if you blink, you miss fall here."

"I was just thinking that. We probably have a week at most before the first wave of tourists rolls in."

"Already? God. It sneaks up on me every year."

"I used to count down the days," I tell her, smiling. "As stressful as running the toy store at Christmas was, I thrived. I woke up every day excited to go to work. Don't get me wrong, I was pissed as all hell at Felix because I wanted my bakery, but I was still happy."

"Do you think you'll go back now?"

Shay looks surprised when I shake my head.

"I don't have a place there anymore. I'm sure I'll help for a few days just before Christmas; everyone chips in then, but Felix has everything under control. Or Abigail does, and he's just doing as he's told." It hurts less than I thought it would, realizing I'm not needed at The Enchanted Workshop right now. There's no Enchanted Bakery to need me anymore. For the first time in a long time, I'm technically not needed. I know I'll grow tired of it, but it feels nice for now.

"How are you feeling about the bakery?" Shay asks. "Do you think you're going to reopen?"

"I feel… relieved. And I feel guilty for feeling relieved,

because I appreciate how much support everyone has given me, and I know people are losing their jobs, but I'm not happy. So, no, I'm not reopening." Saying it feels better than the first gulp of fresh air after getting out of the smoke. It's like the weight of the world just falls off my shoulders with three words: "I'm not reopening."

I know there's more to it than just saying the words—I still own the building, and I have to figure out what I'm going to do with the charred remains of the bakery, but that's a job for once we know what caused the fire, and once I know what my insurance is going to cover.

"I'm proud of you," Shay says, winding her arms around me and kissing my temple. "You don't have to feel guilty, but I know that's easier said than done. You made something amazing with The Enchanted Bakery, but if you're not happy, then it's time to move on. Do you know what you might want to do next?"

"I want to bake," I confirm. That's the one thing I don't have to wonder about. "I wouldn't even mind running the kitchen side of a bakery, I just don't want to do it all, you know? The café side, the admin, the people-ing. I don't know, I guess I'll keep an eye on jobs in Jackson. The commute isn't ideal, but I'll figure it out."

Shay hums, and, when I look her over, she looks nervous.

"What?" I ask.

"I have a suggestion. And you can say no—there's no pressure either way."

"Alright."

She takes a deep breath. "I really liked working together on the movie. And, as far as I can tell, you did too."

"I did."

"Exactly. You want to bake more, and I want to interact with people more. We know we work well together, so... Why don't we work together?"

I can't hide the shock on my face. "You want me to come work at *Épices et Sucré*?"

Shay sits up straight. "Yes. No. Kind of? I want to rebrand, and not just because no one in this town except Rora can actually pronounce the name correctly—you included, for the record."

"Hey!"

"But also," she continues, "it's not the best fit for the town, anyway. I don't think we need to be entirely Christmas themed, but something a little cozier, you know? And I understand if you just don't want the responsibility of running a bakery full stop, but I thought maybe if we did it together—"

"Yes."

The word slips out before I even have time to think about it. But I don't need to think about it. It's the perfect solution for both of us to be happy in Wintermore, and the perfect solution so we don't have to miss working together. I can't believe I didn't even consider it.

Shay blinks. "Oh. I had a whole spiel prepared—I didn't realize it would be so easy. Are you sure, *mon délice*?"

"I'm sure," I say. "It didn't occur to me that I didn't have to give up my dream entirely—and I think I'd enjoy it a lot more if I was sharing it with you. No, I know I would. But are you sure you want to rebrand? *Épices et Sucré* was you and Georgie's thing."

"That's exactly why I need to rebrand. I made the patisserie that Georgie wanted to own one day. It was never what I wanted. I want to do something here in town to honor her. With Nico, maybe, if I can convince him to talk about her. But I don't have to dedicate my life to honoring her."

"You don't," I agree. "But being happy and living the life you want... I think she'd see that as honoring her memory, even if it's not exactly what you talked about when you were younger. You're a good sister, sweetheart. Whatever happens after all of this, wherever she is, I bet she's so proud of you."

She drags in a ragged breath, her eyes watery, and squeezes my hand. "I wish she'd gotten to meet you."

"Me too," I say, wiping a tear as it spills down her cheek. "While we're already emotional, I wasn't entirely honest with you the other day."

"Oh?"

"When I said I thought I was falling for you," I explain, my heart racing. "I know it's way too soon, but we could've died yesterday, so I'm not going to wait until it's more socially acceptable. Sweetheart, I've been crazy about you since that first kiss. I love you." Another three words I've been desperate to say; another relief as I finally put them out into the universe, as I watch them sink into Shay.

"Noelle," she breathes, her tears falling hard and fast now. "I love you, too. So much."

"And to be clear—not casually, right? Not just friends?" I joke, my voice watery.

Shay clasps my face, laughing as I dry her face with the corner of my blanket. "I think, actually, you might just be my best friend. But there's nothing casual about how much I love you—I'm going to keep you forever, if you'll let me."

Forever sounds pretty damn sweet to me.

34

SHAY

ONE MONTH LATER

I t's only been a few weeks since I braced myself, called Nico, and said Georgie's name to him for the first time in twenty-something years. He took it better than expected; I think he knew it was coming. It's impossible not to see how much I've changed in the past two months, but I can't truly move forward without acknowledging what brought me here in the first place.

"I want to do something to honor Georgie in town," I told Nico, after he got over the initial shock of me calling rather than texting.

For a moment, he said nothing; I couldn't even hear him breathing down the line, but I knew he hadn't hung up. And because I'm god-awful with silence, I kept going:

"Maybe plant a tree, or a flower garden, or, I don't know, get a new swing for the playground, or—"

"A bench," he interrupted, surprising me so much I almost dropped my phone.

"A bench?"

"Yeah. I want to make her a bench." His voice was thicker than usual, still gruff and scratchy, but with a softness that made me wonder if he was holding back tears, thinking about her.

"That sounds great. I'll talk to the mayor, but I'm sure she won't have a problem with us putting a bench somewhere."

"I don't know Wintermore very well. Is there a spot you think G"—he sucked in a deep breath—"Georgie. Is there a spot you think she would've liked?"

Hearing him say her name for the first time in so long almost knocked the wind out of me, but I pushed down the tears choking me up and said, "Yeah. I know the perfect place."

I figured a bench would take at least a couple of months to complete, but last night, while Noelle was holding Croissant up to the fridge to "show him things he's never seen before," I got a three-word text:

> It's finished. Tomorrow?

I lean against my car, half-expecting Nico not to show—he never did come back down to meet Noelle after the fire—but, sure enough, an engine rumbles up the road and his truck pulls in beside me.

He steps down from the truck, wearing a red flannel and jeans that look like they've been through surgery a time or two. "Hey."

"Hey!"

Nico frowns at my sweater. "Is that a Christmas sweater?"

I follow him around to the back of the truck. "Yeah. The Whittens don't celebrate Thanksgiving—they celebrate 'pre-Christmas.'" It was heavily implied that the festive dress code wasn't optional.

Nico pauses. "Today is Thanksgiving?"

I nod, not surprised that he wouldn't know. Sometimes I think he would forget Christmas if I didn't brave the mountain to spend the day with him. I don't think he could ever forget our birthday, though.

We were never a big Thanksgiving family growing up, but

Georgie loved the holiday for exactly one reason: after Thanksgiving dinner, every year, our parents let her put up the Christmas tree. Like the Whittens, she would've had a tree year-round if they'd let her. Today feels like the perfect day to honor her.

Nico looks down, his jaw set. He sniffs exactly once before squaring his shoulders. "Good. Yeah. She'd like that."

"She would," I agree, squeezing his arm.

The bench is covered by a blue tarp and some kind of thick bungee cord, presumably to stop the tarp from flying off on Nico's journey down the mountain. He looks at me skeptically when I offer to help him carry it, understandably, considering he has a full foot of height on me, and a hell of a lot more muscle. He single-handedly lifts the bench down, straining but not uncomfortably, and politely pretends I'm helping when I grip the other side to help him carry it to the reservoir.

I marked out the spot I had in mind before he got here, and it fits perfectly, right beside a flat rock that could be a side table if someone was sitting here with a cup of coffee or, knowing Wintermore, peppermint hot chocolate.

Nico fusses with the bench until it's perfectly in place, then stands back and nods. "Good spot."

"I thought so. Can I see it?"

"Oh. Right, of course."

Nico unclips the cords and tosses them aside, and I gasp as he reveals the bench. It's beautiful, like everything he makes, but it's... us. Three little mice stand on top of the backrest, each with a letter carved on their stomachs—N, S, and G. Carved forget-me-nots wind around the arms of the bench, coming up on one side so there's a single flower in front of Georgie's mouse.

"It's beautiful," I say, wiping my eyes. It's no use—the tears are going to fall whether I wipe them or not. "Seriously. You've outdone yourself. How the hell did you do this in less than a month?"

He shifts, rubbing the back of his neck. "I started it twenty years ago. Just wasn't ready to finish it."

I look up at him. His eyes are red, and he looks so much younger.

"But you're ready now?"

He rubs his hand over his beard. "Shit, I don't know, Shay. I don't know if I'll ever be ready." Because he knows as well as I do that this isn't about a bench—it's about closure. It's about moving forward. "But you were ready. I could tell. And I wanted to do it for you."

"Thank you."

If he could hug me after the fire, surely I can hug him now. I wrap my arms around him and, after a second, he does the same. There's still something—someone—missing from the hug, but a soft breeze blows through my hair, and I let myself believe that it's the universe's way of telling us Georgie is still with us.

"Should we test it out?" I ask when we break apart.

"Test what? It's a perfectly good bench. It's not going to break."

I hold my hands up, fighting a laugh at Nico's indignation. "Hey, no one is implying otherwise. I meant test the spot."

"Oh. Right. Sure."

We sit side by side on the bench and stare out at the crystal-clear water. It's a beautiful day—the scent of fresh pine emanates from the forest, the sky is clear, and the air is cool, but not cold. The peace of it all quietens my mind; it's easy to be just in the moment here.

"This was a good choice," Nico says quietly. "Why here?"

"Oh, you know. Georgie loved water so much. I come here a lot, and I can imagine that if she had made it to Wintermore, this would be her favorite spot, too. Also, I get a good view of the mountains from here. It's not like I can see your cabin or anything, but I feel closer to you when I'm here."

I feel Nico looking at me, but I keep my eyes glued to the horizon, because I really don't want him to see me crying again.

He lifts his arm, pointing to the mountain. "Do you see that tall, crooked tree? It kind of pokes out above all the others."

It takes me a second—my eyesight isn't what it used to be, but I spot it eventually. "I see it."

"My cabin isn't too far from that one. There's a lookout there. You can't see it from here, but you can see the town from the lookout. You can see the water. I go there a lot, spend a couple hours looking down, wondering what you're up to. It makes me feel closer to you, too."

There's no hiding the tears streaming down my cheeks when I do look up and meet his eye. The pain in his expression is like a knife in my chest, but if there's one thing I've learned since Georgie died, it's that there's nothing I can do to bear Nico's pain for him. If I could, I'd do it in a heartbeat. I'd take every drop of pain, every drop of regret, and shoulder it for the rest of my life so he didn't have to.

"I'm so fucking sorry, Shay," he says, and I have to look away when a tear slides down his face. "You moved here for me, and we don't see each other any more than we did before. I want to be the brother you deserve, I just…"

"It's okay. I understand. I know how hard it must be to look at me and see Georgie. I don't blame you. I get it, I promise."

"Is that what you think?" Nico asks. I glance at him, and he looks stunned, his face crumpling when I nod in confirmation. "God, no. It was never you, Shay. I'm so sorry if that's how I've made you feel. It's just… it was my fault."

"No. It was a freak acciden—"

"I was the one who wanted to leave early. If we'd left at the time we planned originally, we would've missed the rockslide," he counters.

"And we might have ended up rear-ended or being struck by fucking lightning, Nico. You can't know that."

"Either way, I was driving. I should've had better control of the car." His voice rises gradually.

"No one could have outdriven a giant boulder."

"Then it should have been me!"

"Nico—"

He stands up and crosses his arms, glaring at the reservoir like it was personally responsible for the accident. "It should've been me. I don't understand why she died and I didn't. It's not fair." His voice fades into nothing, and I watch his shoulders shake as sobs wrack his body.

"It's not fair," I agree, standing up and joining him. I don't touch him, just let him cry it out. "No one should've died, Nico. But Georgie did. And she wouldn't want either of us to waste our lives. She wouldn't want us to shut each other out."

"I don't know how to do anything but waste it," Nico says, his face blotchy. "But I know I need to try. If I can't do it for me, and I can't do it for Georgie, I'm going to try and do it for you," he promises, and it's amazing how much pressure one promise sucks out of my chest. I had no idea I was carrying around quite so much.

"Does that mean we're going to see each other more?"

"Definitely. And I called Bryan. I invited him to come and stay this winter with his husband and... shit, I can't even remember his daughters' names."

"Celeste and Sloane," I remind him, bursting with pride. I don't want to make a big deal of it—god knows Nico doesn't like a fuss—but this is the biggest step I've seen him take since Georgie died. "That's amazing. I'll need to drive up when they're here."

"I'd like that," Nico says, a tentative smile curving his lips. "How is the bakery progressing?"

I recognize his need to change the subject onto a lighter note and take it, gratefully.

"Amazing. We're having our grand reopening tomorrow, actually." An idea takes hold, and I open my mouth without thinking it through. "You know, I'm going to the Whittens' for their pre-Christmas dinner tonight, and I'm sure they'd be happy to have you. You could stay tonight and come to the reopening tomorrow."

Nico shoves his hands in his pockets, and I wait for him to let me down gently. "I can't stay—I have the dogs," he says.

"Shit, of course. I forgot about them."

"Understandable—the three of you have never gotten along," he replies, his mustache twitching. "Tomorrow—what time is your reopening?"

"Ten."

Nico nods, his face lighter than I've seen in a long time. "I know I missed when you first opened the patisserie, but I'm not going to miss any more. I'll be there."

35

NOELLE

I'm starting to think that Shay seriously undersold her board game abilities. Since we made things official, she's joined me at every family dinner, most of which end with a board game. The only time she lost was last weekend, when we'd been up since three a.m. because we had to drive to Cheyenne to pick up the new bakery sign, because there was a delay and they couldn't ship it to us in time. A thirteen-hour round trip, and she still came second.

Pre-Christmas is the official start of the Christmas season in our house—we celebrate year-round, of course, but Rora's birthday always falls a few days before Thanksgiving, so we don't go full out until after that. I was sure the Christmas board games would foil her, but she takes first place in Christmas-themed Scrabble with seemingly zero effort, and she's never been sexier than when she plays JINGLES for 119 points.

She fits in with my family like she was always supposed to be here. It helps that they've been spending a lot of time together. No one was surprised to hear that I wouldn't be reopening The Enchanted Bakery, or that Shay and I were going to be working together going forward. Apparently, it wasn't a secret how miserable I was running the bakery. My family was giving me space but planning an intervention for after Christmas if I was still so unhappy.

I'm not.

My parents and Uncle Henry (and Sunny) have been amazing, splitting their time between helping Shay and me set up the new bakery and helping out at The Enchanted Workshop now that the Christmas season is in full swing. Rora took a last-minute job at a local ski lodge, covering for their photographer for a couple of weeks, to get away from the festivities. That's not to say she hasn't helped with our new bakery; she single-handedly designed our new branding, website, and did a beautiful photoshoot for us. And, though she might complain about Wintermore at this time of year, she still showed up to pre-Christmas dinner and dutifully put on the "Mrs. Claus" sweater that my mom handed her.

It's clearly a not-so-subtle hint, considering my uncle Henry's matching "Santa Claus" sweater. I know my parents are dying for them to get married, mostly because they want Rora to legally be a Whitten. Both Rora and Uncle Henry have been going by Stanley-Whitten since Sunny was born, but I don't think either of them is in a rush to plan a wedding, especially not if they're trying to have another baby. I'm surprised they haven't eloped, to be honest.

When Rora and my uncle Henry continue to dodge the hints my parents are dropping their way, Shay and I become their targets. Shay, mostly.

"Have you ever been married, Shay?" my mom asks, and Rora snorts, probably just happy the attention isn't on her anymore.

"I got divorced four years ago, but I was married for seventeen years."

"Seventeen?" Felix says, his jaw practically on the floor. "Damn. I can't imagine being with someone that long."

"Yeah, no shit." Rora tosses a pillow at him.

Shay doesn't seem to mind—she's used to Felix at this point.

As she's telling my parents about Philippe, Felix leans over and whispers, "You would've been nine when Shay got married."

"Right," I reply. "So that's one year older than Abigail was when you graduated high school."

His face turns scarlet, and I snuggle into Shay's side, satisfied. Do I feel a little bad that Felix clearly has the biggest crush of his life on the one person he absolutely can't have without ruining his relationship with his best friend? Of course I do. On the other hand… I'm his sister—if I don't humble him, who will?

I yawn, and Shay looks over at me, her gray eyes reflecting the twinkling Christmas tree lights. "Sleepy, *mon délice*?"

"A little," I admit.

"You two should head up to bed. Big day tomorrow," my dad says, and I'm on my feet, tugging Shay toward the stairs, bidding everyone goodnight, before he's finished speaking.

My parents don't insist that we all stay on holidays, but they like it when we do. Even Rora, Uncle Henry, and Sunny, who live across the street, are staying.

I took most of my stuff with me when I moved, so my childhood bedroom is mostly old trinkets and *Grey's Anatomy* posters I've had since I was twelve.

Shay peruses the room, no doubt cataloguing the alarming number of Addison posters. She looks at me, eyebrow raised.

"She was my lesbian awakening."

"Good choice," Shay hums. "Alanis Morrisette for me. I lost my virginity at a house party my junior year of high school on an inflatable couch listening to 'You Oughta Know.'"

"I couldn't have guessed any part of that sentence. Jesus," I say after laughing so hard my abs hurt. "Damn, that's a much better story than mine. Also junior year, but a plain old bed—not that one, I got a new one when I graduated college—listening to her One Direction playlist. She cried for three hours after and called her mom to come pick her up at like two a.m. because she was homesick." It's no wonder that Mayor Blackwood doesn't like me.

"Three hours? Damn." Shay peers at my bed. "Did you bring a lot of people back here before me?"

"Oh sure," I say, sitting on the edge of the bed. She steps closer, and I spread my legs so she can tuck herself between them. "As I'm sure you've noticed, Wintermore is full of queer women, and they're all breaking my door down to get to me."

"I'd like to see them try," Shay says, leaning down and brushing her nose against my jaw. My head falls back, my eyes fluttering closed. "You're all mine, and I don't plan to give you up."

"You better not," I say, luxuriating in her answering laugh as it vibrates over my skin.

She kisses me, and she tastes like chocolate and coffee liqueur, sweet and syrupy. Standing above me, she has complete control of the pace of our kiss, and she's taking it so fucking slow. Every brush of her tongue against mine is intentional, languid, and it's driving me out of my mind.

Shay pulls back and lifts my sweater over my head, then my shirt, and I start to question if this is a good idea, given how much I'm already struggling to stay quiet.

Her fingers ghost over my skin, tickling and teasing, and I have to bite down on my lip when her mouth follows their path.

"Speaking of forever," she murmurs against my skin. I feel every word reverberating across my collarbone. "What your parents were talking about earlier—"

"Oh my god, please ignore them. They're antsy because they want Rora and my uncle Henry to get married, that's all."

"They don't want to?" Shay asks, unclipping my bra and sliding it from my body.

"They do—fuck. Do we have to talk about this while you have your tongue all over me?"

I feel her lips curve up in a smile against my breast. "I can stop."

"You better not," I gasp. "Okay, yeah, they do want to get married. They're just focused on having another baby first."

Shay hums, and I clench my fists as sparkles appear behind my eyelids. "Makes sense. What about you?"

"What about me?"

She nudges me backward so I'm lying on the bed, and the ends of her hair brush against my naval as she descends, kissing lower and lower.

"Do you want to get married?"

I can't believe she expects me to be able to concentrate, let alone carry on a conversation, *this* conversation, when she's gripping my thighs like that.

"Um, yes? Yes, I do. But it's also not a dealbreaker for me if you don't want to get married again. Not that I think you want to marry *me* or anything, but—"

"I do."

She gives me about half a second to process that before she pushes my jeans down, my underwear aside, and drags her tongue through my lips, flicking the tip over my clit.

"Oh my god," I groan, grabbing a pillow and practically smothering myself with it.

Shay seems to take my muffling solution as a challenge, increasing the speed and pressure of her tongue. I reach for her, my fingers gripping her hair, my legs closing around her. Shay moans, and I find myself rolling my hips without even meaning to, fucking her face.

She teases my entrance with her tongue, pressing the tip inside me while she pushes her thumb firmly on my clit. I don't know how she's learned my body so well, so quickly, but she plays me like I'm an instrument, and she's a prodigy. Every single brush of her fingers, every touch of her tongue, feels intentional, designed specifically to undo me, stitch by stitch.

My body is burning, Shay's touch consuming me. But not so much that my mind isn't playing two words on repeat:

"I do."

She wants to get married. She wants to marry *me*, specifically. The thought tips me over the edge—well, I suppose it's more a combination of the woman I love wanting to marry me, and the same woman pressing two fingers inside me, closing her mouth around my clit, and humming.

I break apart like glass, crying into the pillow, my back bowing off the bed. Shay drags her tongue over me, slowing but not stopping her fingers as they massage inside me.

"Je suis tellement putain d'obsédée par ton goût." I swear I almost come again as the French falls from her lips.

Shay pulls me back together, coaxing me down from my high with soft kisses against my clit. My body goes limp, my legs slipping down her back, and I drop the pillow, drawing in a deep breath.

Shay sits back, and I push myself up on my elbows, trying to catch my breath.

"Shay."

"What?"

"You can't just tell someone you want to marry them, then go down on them and give them a mind-blowing orgasm with no explanation."

She holds her hands up, gesturing to me. "Clearly, I can."

A quiet laugh falls from her lips at my stunned expression, and she stands, leaning over me, her lips almost close enough to kiss.

"Did you mean it?" I ask, my heart hammering.

She gives me one chaste kiss and climbs up on the bed, lying with her head on the pillow, and patting the spot beside her. I'd be embarrassed by the sheer amount of effort it takes me to lie beside her if she weren't the one who had turned my bones to Jell-O.

"Of course I mean it," she answers, playing with the ends of my hair. The purple is faded, and I rarely do the same color twice in a row, but purple is Shay's favorite color, so it's staying. "Why wouldn't I want to marry you? *Je t'aime, mon délice.*"

"Hey, I know that one!" I joke, and she snorts, her eyes glimmering.

I also know the nickname now—my curiosity got the better of me, and I looked it up: "my delight," she calls me. If I'd known that's what it meant the first time she said it, there would've been no chance of me pretending I wanted to be *friends*.

"A lot of people don't want to get remarried after they get divorced," I point out.

"True. But I'd like to know how it feels to be married to the person I'm supposed to be married to," she replies, like it's the easiest thing in the world. "I assume you want a Christmas-themed wedding." She assumes correctly. "And this Christmas is probably a little soon, but that gives me plenty of time to plan the most outlandish proposal you could possibly think of." Her eyes are so bright; how did I go so long without noticing the way she glows?

"What if I want to be the one to propose?" I ask, and she screws up her mouth.

"Hmm. I suppose we could do that cute thing where we accidentally propose at the same time. As long as you say yes, I don't really care when or how it happens."

I press my forehead to hers, murmuring, "I'll say yes," against her lips, then lose myself in my favorite flavor.

36

NOELLE

An electrical fault. That's all it took to turn The Enchanted Bakery to ash—one little electrical fault, likely caused by a leak after the storm we had the night of the wrap party. It's a reminder that everything is so fucking fragile.

At least my insurance is paying out.

Rebuilding the charred remains is going to take months, if not longer. Shay and I considered waiting and funneling all our energy into rebuilding so we could open a bigger bakery with a bigger kitchen space, but neither of us wants to go so long without baking. We'll fix it up eventually, but for now, we've cleared everything out and closed off the main floor. Shay and I decided to take a risk by keeping most of The Enchanted Bakery's staff, and they'll work out of the basement kitchen, which is still in perfect condition, thanks to the expensive-ass fire door I invested in when I first renovated the bakery. According to Quinn, that fire door is the reason the fire didn't make it into the stairway —that door is probably the reason Shay and I are still alive. Worth every penny.

My apartment is also unscathed, and we hired a company to come in and professionally clean it and the basement kitchen of any ash and smoke residue. Technically, I've been free to move back in for weeks. But, by some unspoken agreement, neither Shay nor I has brought it up.

We've barely stopped working since we set an opening date for our new—shared—bakery, but I don't mind working all the time when it's something I'm genuinely excited about. And when I get to do it with her.

Physical labor aside, the whole process has been surprisingly easy. I expected it to feel like a mountain when Shay and I sat down to list everything that was important to us, but we were completely aligned. She mostly wants to work out front in the café, interacting with people, but still wants to take on custom cake orders and help out with decorating where needed. I want to work in the back, developing new recipes, and, like Shay, work on custom orders.

So, we turned her kitchen into a custom-order kitchen, and most of the staff staying on from The Enchanted Bakery will be working on the bigger batches of things for parties, mail orders, and the café itself. Gracie will be handling the bulk of our admin, we've promoted one of my bakers to kitchen manager, and we have a couple of bakers who'll be working with us in the smaller kitchen.

Perhaps most importantly, Shay and I will never be more than twenty feet away from each other while we're working together. It's the perfect setup.

I lean against the counter and watch her straighten the star on top of the tree in the window. Right now, it's a Christmas tree, but Shay insisted that, if we're leaving it up year-round, we have to update the decorations seasonally. As long as there's Christmas lights, I'm not complaining—and there are a *lot* of Christmas lights in here. Wintermore can be pretty dreary in the cooler months, but with the flick of a switch, tens of thousands of Christmas lights glow and twinkle all over the ceiling. We painted the ceiling a pretty pale yellow, and, inspired by Shay's locket, painted a gold letter to represent all of the people who helped us get where we are today: my parents, Felix, Rora, my uncle Henry, Sunny, Nico, and Georgie. And at the center of the ceiling, in a swirly heart, Shay freehanded: N + S. If you didn't know they were there, you'd never spot them.

"How does that look?" Shay asks, peering over her shoulder.

"Perfect, sweetheart."

She smiles, dusting her hands off on her apron and crossing the café toward me, pausing every other second to straighten a chair or wipe a completely crumb-free table.

"Quit fussing. Everything is perfect," I say as she reaches me. I pull her into me, sliding my hands into the back pockets of her jeans. "And the line of people waiting outside is going to think so, too."

Her eyes widen. "There's a line?"

"There's a line," I confirm. "Why don't you get everyone out from the back, and I'll go and let them in?"

Shay nods, pressing a quick kiss to my lips before heading for the door that separates the café from the kitchen.

"Love you, by the way," she calls over behind herself, disappearing before I can reply.

I walk toward the front door with a wide smile and nothing but excitement for our new chapter. It's funny to think that three months ago, I dreaded this walk every morning. I saw the lines and felt my heart sink, because I knew it meant I'd be rushed off my feet all day and wouldn't get to bake. Back then, I had to force myself out of bed every morning and drag myself downstairs.

Now, I wake up in Shay's arms, usually when Croissant decides it's time for his breakfast and demonstrates by whacking our faces with his paws. Now, I see the line outside and feel proud of the bakery Shay and I have built together, not alone, but with my family and our team. Now, I know I'll be leaving at a reasonable time, with the woman I love, and taking at least two days off a week, because I'm not trying to figure everything out without asking for help.

I guess fall really is the season of change.

I unlock the front door and pull it open, ready to greet our first visitors—my parents, naturally. There's never been a time when they weren't first in line for something me, Felix, or Rora was doing.

"Welcome," I say, stepping back, but my dad sweeps me into a hug.

"Proud of you, kiddo. Always, but especially today."

My mom tugs him away, which is just as well, because I'm not above crying. Rora and Uncle Henry follow, and Sunny is wearing a T-shirt, hand embroidered by her dad, with our new bakery logo on it.

"Future employee of the month right there," I say, tapping her on the nose, before turning to greet the next person in line.

Of course, I know everyone here. This is the town that raised me, that supported me when I sang "The Twelve Days of Christmas" in the Christmas pageant when I was nine, and when I opened The Enchanted Bakery last year, but they're not just congratulating *me* on opening the new bakery.

"This looks amazing, Noelle. You and Shay have outdone yourselves."

"Wow, you can really see the perfect blend of both of you in here."

Mayor Blackwood gives me a small smile as she approaches. "I don't know what to congratulate you on more—the bakery, or Shay."

"Both make me pretty happy, but Shay is my favorite."

"I take full credit for bringing you two together," she says, and I don't bother hiding my laugh.

"I'd expect nothing less, Mayor Blackwood."

Her gaze rakes over me. "Really, Noelle. You've both done

amazing things for this town. And I think you're probably old enough to call me Angela."

Surprised, I return her smile. "Thank you. Angela."

We both wrinkle our noses. "Too weird," I say, and she agrees, heading into the bakery with a wave.

It's amazing how many people have shown up for us, but it's the tall figure that hovers at the back of the line, approaching only when there's no one else left, that I'm happiest to see.

"Hey, Nico," I say. I step outside because the café is bustling, and that has to be overwhelming for someone who spends all their time on a mountain with only dogs and wildlife for company. "It's good to see you again. I'm so glad you could make it."

"Hi," he says. His lips lift in a strained smile, but despite how different his haunted expression is from his sister's, I see so much of Shay in him. He looks older than her. His eyes are a darker gray, his hair and beard dark brown, but they have the same sharp nose, almond eyes, and thick lashes. He holds his mouth in the same way she does, and he stands with his head tilted left ever so slightly, exactly like Shay.

"This is amazing," he says, gesturing to the bakery. "I can't believe you pulled it together so fast."

"It's been a surprisingly smooth process," I admit.

"Still, it looks good. I'm happy for you. Both for the bakery, and for you and Shay."

"Thanks, Nico. I'm happy for us, too."

Speak of the devil, I hear footsteps coming toward us, and I know before she speaks that it's Shay.

"You made it!"

She hugs him, and his face softens as he hugs her back, making him look ten years younger.

"This is incredible. You did good," he tells her when they break apart, and her face lights up.

"Thank you." She wraps her arm around my waist, almost like she needs to steady herself.

Nico clears his throat, looking at his shoes. "I made you something. Both of you." He reaches into a bag I hadn't noticed and pulls out a carved wooden boat. "Shay told me about your picnic on the boat—she sent me a couple of pictures, and I thought it'd be a nice memory for the two of you to have," he adds, shifting uncomfortably.

The boat is maybe ten inches at the most, and I gasp as I take in the details. Two figures, sitting across from each other, with a tiny cat sitting between them. How he's managed to make everything so clear and detailed when it's so small, I have no idea.

"That is… Holy shit. I don't even know what to say." I shake my head in disbelief at how beautiful the carving is. It's wild that such a large man who looks like he wrestles bears for fun created something so perfect, so delicate.

"It's amazing, Nico. You really do blow me away," Shay says, sounding a little choked up.

"Thank you," I tell him, as he presses the boat into my hands. "It's… Wow."

"It's nothing," he says, and I get the feeling he might turn around and bolt if we don't wrap things up.

Shay must notice too, because she changes the subject. "Do you want to come in and get something to eat and drink? I know it's busy, so it's totally fine if not. I can bring something out for you."

"No, I want to see it. I'll be fine." He squares his shoulders, and Shay blinks, surprised.

"Alright. Well, after you." Nico walks on ahead, and I breathe a sigh of relief when Rora and my uncle Henry meet him by the door. I know they probably know him better than anyone in town, besides Shay.

I start to follow, but Shay holds me back.

"Hey. Can we just stay here for a second?" she asks. "I feel like I haven't had time to take it all in."

"I know, right? It's so busy. A good busy, though," I add, wrapping my arms around her and resting my chin on her head.

"A very good busy."

We both stare up at the shop sign, quietly taking it all in.

"Who would've thought," I murmur. "You and me."

"Me and you. We build something pretty amazing, *mon délice,*" she says, and I know she's not just talking about the bakery.

"I love you, sweetheart. I'm so happy we get to do this together. I'm so happy we get to have a life together."

She turns in my arms so she can stand on her tiptoes to kiss me. "Me too. I love you so much." She takes a deep breath. "Okay. Let's head back in there."

We walk hand in hand back into the bakery, our bakery, and I glance up at the sign one last time as we pass under it:

SPICY OR SWEET

The French Stuff

Mon délice.
My delight.

J'ai passée une incroyable soirée. Tu es toujours magnifique,
mais espécialement quand tu t'effondres pour moi.
I had an amazing time last night. You're always beautiful, but
especially when you fall apart for me.

Tu me donnes l'impression d'être au paradis. Encore. S'il te plaît.
You feel like heaven. More. Please.

Je suis tellement putain d'obsédée par ton goût.
I'm so fucking obsessed with the taste of you.

Je t'aime.
I love you.

The Spicy Stuff

If you should, for whatever reason, wish to revisit *just* the spicy moments… you'll find no judgment here! But you will find the spicy scenes here:

- Chapter Fourteen
- Chapter Sixteen
- Chapter Seventeen
- Chapter Twenty
- Chapter Twenty-six
- Chapter Twenty-nine
- Chapter Thirty-five

Enjoy!

The Sweet Stuff

APPLE AND AMARETTO CARAMEL PIE
WITH CARDAMOM WHIPPED CREAM

- 5 - 6 Granny Smith apples, peeled, sliced thinly
- The juice of 1/2 a lemon
- 1/3 cup white sugar
- 1/3 cup brown sugar
- 1/2 teaspoon cinnamon
- 1/4 teaspoon nutmeg
- Pinch of salt

1. Mix together and let sit for 10-15 mins.
2. Put mixture in strainer over a bowl for a further 10-15 mins to drain the apple juice.
3. Pour juice into a pan, bring to a boil, simmer for 5-6 minutes, then turn off the heat.
4. Add 2 tablespoons of butter/vegan butter and whisk until the mixture is smooth and thick.
5. Let the mixture cool for 5 mins before adding 1 tablespoon of amaretto (for an alcohol free option, skip this or add a dash of almond extract.)
6. Mix caramel and apples, and pour into your pie crust.
7. Cover your pie with strips of pie crust in a lattice style,

press down the edges with a fork, and trim off the
excess.

8. Brush the pie with milk/plant milk of your choice.
    Optional: sprinkle with cinnamon sugar.
9. Bake at 425°f/225°c for 25-35 minutes, until the pie is
    nicely browned. Keeping an eye on the edges and
    cover with foil if they start to burn.

- 1 cup whipping cream (dairy or plant based)
- 1 teaspoon powdered sugar
- 1 teaspoon vanilla
- 1/2 teaspoon ground cardamom
- A pinch of salt

Combine and whip to medium peaks. If you're using a thinner
plant based cream, adding an extra teaspoon of powdered sugar
can help thicken the cream.

Add whipped cream to your pie when serving.

Use any extra cream sensibly.

Acknowledgments

So many people helped bring Noelle and Shay's love story to life, and I'm so grateful to each and every one of them.

Thank you to my husband Kyle and our sweet baby Pumpkin for all the forehead kisses (Kyle) and bites (Pumpkin,) and keeping me sane-ish while writing. Thank you to Claire, the Rora to my Noelle, who tries her best to convince me not to overwork myself. I don't listen, but I appreciate it anyway.

Thank you to my incredible PA Danie for many things, but especially for inspiring the whisk scene. Thank you to my agent, Amanda at SBR Media, Katie at Between The Covers Editorial, Ellie at Love Notes PR, Cassidy Hudspeth Editing, Dominique Davis, Siân at Books of a Ginger, and Freddie M. Translations for all your help.

Thank you to my amazing street team—Abigail, Aimee, Allie, Ashley, Caitlin, Charlie, Claire, Danie, Demi, Elena, Jenna. Jessica, Karina, Kate, Lil, Molly, Rebecca, Sarah, Sophie D., and Sophie L. And to my beta readers—Claire, Danie, Effy, Emily, Molly, Paige, Parker, and Rae. I feel so lucky to have you all!

And to my readers… Thank you. Seriously. You changed my life with the love you showed Naughty or Nice. Sophie of last year would never in a million years have believed the opportunities that would come her way because of one little Santa kink, and a bunch of amazing, enthusiastic readers cheering her on. I'm so grateful to all one of you. Thank you!

Love,
Sophie

Sophie Snow lives in Scotland with her husband and cat, Pumpkin (who she loves dearly, even if he does bite.)

She writes spicy romance books with messy, queer characters and too many Taylor Swift references to count. She has been in love with love stories for as long as she can remember, and writing them as songs and novels since she was twelve.

A forest fairy in a past life, Sophie loves spending time in nature, drinking too much coffee, and trying out more hobbies than she can keep up with.

You can find more from Sophie by visiting her website at www.sophiesnowbooks.com, or scanning this QR code: